SINK THE TIRPITZ

SINK THE TIRPITZ

Duncan Harding

SEVERN
SH
HOUSE

This first world edition published
in Great Britain 1996 by
SEVERN HOUSE PUBLISHERS LTD of
9–15 High Street, Sutton, Surrey SM1 1DF.
First published in the U.S.A. 1996 by
SEVERN HOUSE PUBLISHERS INC. of
595 Madison Avenue, New York, NY 10022.

British Library Cataloguing in Publication Data
Harding, Duncan
   Sink the Tirpitz
   1. English fiction – 20th century
   I. Title
   823.9′14 [F]

ISBN 0-7278-4923-9

Typeset by Hewer Text Composition Services, Edinburgh.
Printed and bound in Great Britain by
Hartnolls Ltd, Bodmin, Cornwall.

Withernsea, N. Humberside

'Arthur Horace Hurry of North Road, Withernsea, Yorks, has reported making a curious discovery yesterday. The amateur angler was out fishing in his cobble *Storm Two*, some 20 miles off the Yorkshire Coast, when his net dragged up what appeared to be a piece of old copper plate. Copper being valuable scrap, Mr Hurry took the plate home with the rest of his catch of codling. But after cleaning it he was surprised to find some German writing on the plate, including the words '*KS Tirpitz*'.

The "*Tirpitz*", Germany's largest battleship, was sunk by the RAF in Kaafjord at the back of Altenfjord, Norway, in November 12 1944. How the plate came to be found off the E. Yorks coast remains, therefore, a mystery. Mr Hurry says he will sell it to any collector 'for a couple of tenners'. So you collectors of naval memotabilia out there, here's your chance!'

News Item, *Hull Daily Mail*, 15th July 1995

Prelude to a Murder

November 12, 1944

They came in from the sea. Thirty-eight four-engined Lancasters, heavy, powerful, threatening. Down below, the mountains fringing the Norwegian fjord were already heavy with snow. Here and there tiny fishing hamlets bordered the still, green water, thin plumes of smoke rising from the houses. A road wound in and around the mountains but nothing moved along it. It was as if the remote northern fjord was cut off from the rest of this crazy, war-torn world. But the 200-odd young men flying this attack knew differently. Down there, there were thousands of other young men, who would soon be alerted to their presence and would do their utmost to shoot them from the sky.

Now the strike force began to climb. Young as they were the pilots were all veterans, many from 217 squadron, the Dam Busters. They needed few orders to tell them what to do next. Besides, wireless traffic would only alert the enemy operators listening down below in their cramped steel compartments, tensed to pick up any sign of impending danger.

Up in the lead the Wing Commander, his face wearing a huge sweeping moustache, pressed the switch on his R/T set and spoke into his microphone. "Skipper, here," the crew heard him say, his voice metallic and distorted over the intercom, "skipper here. Can you hear me?"

3

Then he went through the usual pre-attack procedure.

"Rear-gunner?"

"Okay, skipper," came back the answer.

"Mid turret?"

"Turret working out, skipper," was the reply.

"Bloody good show, Nobby. Keep your eyes peeled. They've got FW190s up here and you know those buggers."

"Peeled like tinned tomatoes, skipper!"

Finished with that check, the young Wing Commander trimmed the heavy bomber, laden with its single 12,000 pound Tallboy bomb, and raised his gloved thumb to his co-pilot.

The latter did the same and the two pilots started to search port and starboard for their target. For nearly two years now the Royal Navy had been trying to sink her. Now this day the Royal Air Force was at last going to do their job for them. As the Wing Commander had told his crews at the briefing in Scotland hours before, "The boys in blue, chaps are going to be green with envy." His voice had hardened and his keen eyes had swept the circle of young faces, as if he were committing them to memory for one last time. "Some of us might get the chop on this one. But remember. *This day we are going to sink the West's largest and most powerful battleship!*"

Time passed. Below in the fjord they could just make out two small boats. The Wing Commander frowned and hoped they were Norwegian, not German. If they were the latter they would surely radio their own people that this airborne strike force was on its way. He dismissed the thought. The time for such worries was over. Anyway, the Germans would soon know that they were there.

"Skipper!" An urgent voice cut into his thoughts. It

was his co-pilot, eyes wild with excitement above his oxygen mask as he gestured excitedly downwards.

"What is it, Jumbo?"

"There she is, skipper," the co-pilot answered. "To starboard . . . the *Tirpitz!*"

The Wing Commander craned his neck and gasped. It was indeed the world's greatest battleship, a long grey shape clearly outlined against the startling cold blue of the fjord. "By Christ, Jumbo!" he exclaimed, "and they haven't even got the usual smoke screen in place!" Intelligence had briefed them before take-off that as soon as it was daylight the *Tirpitz* was usually shrouded in a thick smoke screen to deter aerial attackers. Now for some reason the great ship was clearly visible. "Whacko!" the Wing Commander chortled. "Someone is going to get a rocket for that!"

"Right up his arsehole," Jumbo, the co-pilot, answered happily, "– if he survives!"

"For what we are now about to receive, may the Lord make us truly thankful," the Wing Commander intoned with mock solemnity and then he broke radio silence. "To all," he snapped, very businesslike now, "we're going in. Make it quick, but make it precise. Once you've dropped your eggs, scoot. Good luck and good hunting, chaps!" He flicked off the switch and stared down below at the first cherry-red light of the flak, followed an instant later by the glowing streaks of tracer curving upwards, growing in speed by the second. The aircraft rocked. Puffballs of black smoke appeared on both sides of the Lancaster. He trimmed the controls automatically. He had been through this many times before, aware, as he always told himself on these occasions, if your number's up, it's up and there's nothing you can do about it.

The first squadron went into the attack as planned,

while the Wing Commander's plane circled and watched, his body braced against the seat, controls and armrest.

The lead Lancaster staggered and seemed to jump higher into the air. He knew what that meant. The bomb-aimer had released his 'block-buster', the 12,000 lb Tallboy bomb. He counted off the seconds and waited. Suddenly the fjord to port of the *Tirpitz* erupted in a crazy, white, whirling spout of water. For a moment the great battleship disappeared from view as tons of water slammed down on to her superstructure. It cleared and the Wing Commander groaned. The *Tirpitz* was rocking violently, but she was still intact. The bomb had missed. But already the next Lancaster was thundering in, ready for the kill.

"Go on, Peter!" the Wing Commander urged, gripping the controls fiercely, as the second Lancaster soared through a wall of lethal puffballs, weaving to and fro expertly, as the German gunners tried to cone in on him. "Hit the bitch! *Now!*"

As if listening to his unspoken command, the bomb-aimer pulled the lever to open the bomb doors beneath the big four-engined plane. Next moment he pressed the bomb-release tit. As the huge bomb fell from the plane's belly, the aircraft leapt high in the air, freed of that immense 12,000 lb bomb.

In his command plane, the Wing Commander waited tensely, hardly daring to breathe, counting off the seconds in his mind, his eyes fixed hypnotically on the great ship, now ablaze from end to end, as the gunners frantically attempted to knock out the attackers, while sailors scurried back and forth lighting the smoke pots to create the smoke screen.

Suddenly – startlingly – the *Tirpitz* reared up, her stern end out of the water. A great ragged hole appeared in her armoured deck and a mast fell down. Life-rafts and boats went flying over the side and men too into the freezing waters of the fjord.

"By George, Jumbo!" he cried over the intercom, "*We've hit her!*"

As the second plane sped down the fjord, followed on both sides by the angry fire of the German land gunners, the Wing Commander stared at the great ragged hole in *Tirpitz*'s stern, noting that the battleship was already beginning to list.

The third Lancaster came zooming in. Now, the German shipboard gunners were waiting. They turned the full weight of their multiple 105 mm and 37 mm AA fire on the approaching plane. The Lancaster seemed to be flying through a solid wall of black puffballs and angry white tracer. But the bomber appeared to possess a charmed life. Time and time again when the anxious Wing Commander felt the bomber couldn't make it – how could anyone survive that terrible wall of flying steel? – it came through.

But the fire rattled the pilot. The plane shook itself with each close call and the Wing Commander guessed already that the bomb-aimer, who now would be guiding the pilot on to the target, was going to miss – and he did. He released his huge bomb too early. Again a huge fountain of angry water raced to the sky as the bomb struck the fjord, but when it had cleared a disappointed Wing Commander could see that the explosion had done little damage to the target other than bring a cascade of seawater down into it.

The fourth Lancaster went in. But this time the German gunners had got the measure of the attackers. The bombers had made a simple tactical mistake. They were all coming in from the same quarter. As soon as the Lancaster came zooming across the snow-topped mountains, an immense barrage of fire opened up. This Lancaster didn't stand a chance. Suddenly it appeared to hesitate in mid-air as it was hit repeatedly by 105 mm shells. Desperately the frantic pilot tried to keep control but to no avail. The starboard engine exploded. Next instant the wing crumpled and tore away, falling to earth like a great metallic leaf. In a flash the aircraft went out of control.

"For Chrissake, bale out . . . *bale out!*" the Wing Commander yelled. "*Bale—*"

The words died on his lips. In a great ball of angry fire the Lancaster disintegrated. One moment the big four-engined plane was there; the next it was gone. Metal fragments rained down to the water, accompanied by shattered bodies of the eight-man crew.

The Wing Commander reacted immediately. "All right, we'll go in from port, Jumbo." He snapped on the intercom. "Bomb-aimer."

"Skipper," Jacko Jackson, the bomb-aimer, responded immediately.

"Prepare to bomb. We're going to get the bugger this time."

"Yes, skipper," Jacko replied joyfully. "Will there be a putty medal in it for me?"

Despite his frustration, the Wing Commander grinned. Jacko, like the rest of them, were good, reliable lads. "Hit the *Tirpitz* and sink her," he said, "and you can have a whole chestful of 'em. Over and out!"

The lone Lancaster veered away from the remainder of the attack force. For a little while it disappeared behind the high mountains and the German gunners who had been paying some attention to the Wing Commander's plane, realising it was the one which had been controlling the attack, turned their attention to easier targets. Then suddenly it was there again, zooming dangerously low over the rugged peaks, coming in at top speed.

"Bomb doors open," Jacko reported over the intercom, his voice quite calm and controlled.

The Wing Commander nodded to himself. Carefully he held the heading. Once again the *Tirpitz's* gunners turned their full fury on the lone Lancaster. The Wing Commander tried to ignore the massive hail of fire levelled at him, focusing his concentration on his instruments, listening to the commands of the bomb-aimer as he prepared to release that gigantic 12,000 lb bomb.

Like the beak of a giant bird, the flak ripped at the plane's eggshell of metal and perspex. The raven-fear came knocking and knocking. With all his strength the Wing Commander guarded the little crystal core of his will-power. Yet he kept his hands and feet gentle, relaxed in the controls.

"An S-turn to starboard, skipper," the bomb-aimer's voice came over the intercom, eager and determined despite that furious fire from below.

The Wing Commander did as ordered.

"On heading," the bomb-aimer called. "Steady . . . *steady!*"

On both sides of the Lancaster smoke and flame erupted, rocking the big plane from side to side. Still the Wing Commander coaxed it through the buffeting turbulence, keeping that vital little needle central, quite central.

"*Steady . . . steady . . .!*"

The Wing Commander tensed. It couldn't be long now. Below them the *Tirpitz* was a hot, quivering fury of angry flame.

9

Suddenly the Lancaster lurched. "*Bomb gone!*" the bomb-aimer yelled.

Hurriedly the Wing Commander fought the controls and pulled the stick back to gain height and escape. Below, the *Tirpitz* trembled violently like a live thing. Her masts crumpled. Slowly, dramatically, she started to turn turtle.

"Christ Almighty!" Jumbo yelled over the intercom, "We've gone and sunk the frigging *Tirpitz!*" And then they were gone winging their way into the harsh blue sky before the enemy fighters came, leaving the greatest battleship in the West to sink on this November day.

PART ONE

Footprints in the Sand

Chapter One

"Damn this fog," Lieutenant O'Rourke cursed, coughing as the cold wet damp penetrated his throat. "Can't see a hand before your damn eyes!"

"Sea fret or sea rook we calls it in these parts," Chief Petty Officer Harding commented as he stood next to the handsome young skipper, muffled there in his duffle coat with the hood up so that he looked like a hard-faced old nun.

"I don't give a toss what the locals call it, Chiefie," O'Rourke said, as he peered through the mist from the bridge of the powerful 70 ft motor-launch, trying to penetrate the white gloom of the Humber estuary. "For all we know the whole ruddy German fleet could be out there at this very moment. And if we make a muck of this patrol, Howling Mad'll keel-haul the ruddy lot of us."

CPO Harding allowed himself a tight smile. Lieutenant Commander Keith, known behind his back as 'Howling Mad' on account of throwing back his big head and baying like a crazy hound when he was angry (which was often), even frightened him a little. The Squadron Commander was not a man to be crossed.

They crawled on, the motor-launch's props barely stirring the brown, sluggish water of the Humber. Down below they could hear Sparks, the radio operator, singing that he had "*Spurs that jingle-jangle, jingle*" over and over again in a poor imitation of Bing Crosby. Otherwise there was no sound but the muted throb of the engines. They might well have been the last people alive in the world.

Time passed. A rating came up on to the bridge with two chipped mugs. "Cookie thought you might like to have a cuppa cocoa, sir," he said and presented them to the skipper and the CPO. To the latter he gave a sly wink and muttered, "There's a little drop to warm yer cockles in that one, Chiefie."

The CPO accepted the mug as if it was his right and after the rating left growled, "Thieving scouse sod!" He raised the laced cocoa to his lips, but stopped suddenly.

"What is it, Chiefie?" O'Rourke asked urgently, noting the look of alarm on the old man's wizened face.

Harding didn't answer. Instead he cocked his head to the left, pulling down the hood of his duffle coat. "There's something out there, sir," he said after a minute.

"Fishing boat from Brid or Scarborough?"

Harding shook his head. "No, sir. Engines too powerful."

O'Rourke sucked his bottom lip, his handsome young face suddenly thoughtful. "You think—" he began, but Harding beat him to it.

"I do indeed sir," he interrupted. "If yer had spent as much frigging time as I have – if you'll forgive my French, sir – in these waters, you'd know the prevailing wind is a north westerly. So if old Jerry is out there he's coming from a north westerly direction."

O'Rourke nodded his understanding. "I get you, Chiefie. But we haven't seen much of old Jerry, as you call him, for weeks now. He's had it according to the papers. Our chaps are already fighting in Germany

14

and the Russians are doing the same on their eastern borders. The Germans are finished."

CPO Harding pulled at the end of his long, beaked nose and expertly flung the dewdrop hanging there on to the deck of the bridge. "If you've known Jerry as long as I have, fighting the sod in two wars, you'd know he was a cunning bugger. He'll go on to the very end."

"I'll take your word for it, Chiefie," O'Rourke answered, smiling to himself for he knew behind Harding's back the crew said that he had been in the Navy so long that he had fought with Nelson at the Battle of Trafalgar.

His smile vanished and he snapped into the voice tube. "Both ahead!"

"Both ahead," came the answer from the engine-room.

The motor-launch started to pick up speed, with the two men on the bridge peering into the white gloom, trying to spot what might be a German intruder into the Humber, though O'Rourke himself thought it was unlikely. But all the same he had served with the grizzled Chief Petty Officer for nearly a year now and he had come to respect the latter's sea knowledge and experience.

They passed Spurn Point, not that they could see the lighthouse marking the exit of the Humber into the sea. But the sudden turbulence told them that they were now in the North Sea.

They ploughed on, each man on the bridge wrapped up in a cocoon of his own thoughts and apprehensions as they tried to locate the source of the engine noise, both wondering if the Germans might still be attempting to get into the Humber and sink shipping at this stage of the war.

O'Rourke somehow doubted it. After all the *Hull Daily*

Mail had reported only yesterday that the British Second Army was poised to make its dash from the border of the Reich to the Rhine, Germany's last natural barrier, at any moment. What purpose would be served by sinking a few coastal freighters now? Why, they had even lifted the blackout regulations in Hull and soon, according to the BBC, the Home Guard would be stood down.

"Sir." Again Harding cut into his reverie. "Over there to starboard. I think I can see something."

O'Rourke turned in the direction indicated and strained his eyes, narrowing them to slits as he peered through the white gloom, already aware of the soft throb of powerful engines – several of them.

"Stand the watch to, Chiefie," O'Rourke ordered, making a sudden decision.

"Ay, ay, sir," Harding answered in the same instant that the first sinister long shape slid into view, followed a moment later by another.

"Holy cow!" O'Rourke breathed. "E-boats!" They were German high-powered torpedo-boats.

"Two of the sods," Harding agreed as whistles shrilled and the gun-crews came pelting up from below, pulling on their helmets and flash gear as they ran for the gun.

A star shell erupted above them. Immediately the British motor-launch was bathed in the harsh glowing white light of the flare. The Germans had spotted them already.

Behind the bridge the rating manning the twin Vicker machine-guns opened fire. Tracer zipped angrily towards the first of the lean rakish-prowed German craft. Slugs ran the length of her superstructure. A radio mast was hit and it tumbled to the deck, flashing angry blue and red sparks.

The Germans retaliated immediately. Green and red

tracer came streaming towards the motor-launch like swarm of dragonflies, criss-crossing in mid-air and converging on the British craft as the E-boat surged forward, a great white bone in her teeth, heading towards them on a collision course.

Grimly O'Rourke stared at what appeared to be a solid wall of glowing white tracer shells, telling himself that the twin Lewis-guns dating back to World War One would be little use against the modern German quick-firing 20mm Oerlikons, each of which fired nearly 500 shells a minute.

Suddenly his own gun crew, manning the 6 pounder power-operated gun, crashed into action. The deck shivered beneath O'Rourke's feet as the gun thundered and a tracer shell shrieked towards the nearest E-boat. The young gun-layer was accurate. Quite distinctly O'Rourke could hear the thud of his first shell striking home. Next moment the forecastle of the white-painted E-boat disappeared in a thick burst of angry violet flame. The German craft seemed to stop, then rear out of the water, as if it had run into an invisible wall. For a few moments the craft limped on, running out of power all the time, little figures throwing themselves over the sides into the freezing water.

"Hard to port!" O'Rourke yelled urgently into the tube as the dying E-boat headed towards them on a collision course. Perhaps it was out of control. Perhaps the German skipper intended to ram the British craft, O'Rourke didn't know. Hastily he grabbed a stanchion as the motor-launch heeled wildly and then roared up behind the burning E-boat, guns chattering.

The second E-boat took up the challenge. Tracer sped towards the British craft like a myriad of angry red hornets. O'Rourke could hear and feel the shells slamming into the side of the launch. To the left of the armoured bridge the perspex panel shattered into a spider's web. Harding raised his boot and aimed a kick at it, breaking the plastic so that they could see. The E-boat was only yards away, hurtling through the fog, all guns blazing.

"He's going to ram us sir!" the CPO cried above the crazy racket. "*QUICK!*"

There was no time for thought. Instinctively O'Rourke yelled his order. The motor-launch heeled violently. In the very last instant the E-boat slid by them, its bow wave making the motor-launch rock to and fro. Behind the bridge the rating manning the twin Vickers fired at the E-boat's bridge, rattling off two full belts of ammunition at a tremendous rate and the enemy's bridge disappeared in a welter of splintered wood and broken glass. Thick white smoke started to pour from the E-boat.

"Bloody good show!" O'Rourke yelled excitedly. "That'll show 'em!"

It certainly did. The second E-boat had had enough. Slowing down noticeably, smoke pouring from her midships, the E-boat pulled back into the fog. Minutes later it had disappeared, the sound of its engines becoming muted by the mist and then silent.

"What now, sir?" Harding asked. "Follow her?"

"No," O'Rourke answered firmly. "I think we've done enough for this dawn and I don't want to risk the vessel unnecessarily."

The old salt nodded his head in agreement. "Think you're wise, sir. Oldest trick in the world. Let you go chasing after the one, thinking you've got him on the run and there's another sod waiting for you to walk into the trap. For all we know in this fog there could be a whole flotilla of 'em out there."

"Get Sparks to send a signal. *'Engaged two of the enemy. One badly damaged and listing. Last seen on a bearing for Spurn Point'*." O'Rourke looked in the direction the first E-boat had taken after being hit. "Add, *'We're following. Will pick up survivors.'*"

Harding pulled a face. "Wouldn't say that, sir. Howling Mad doesn't like his craft picking up survivors."

O'Rourke gave the old CPO a weary smile. "Well, for, once Chiefie, Howling Mad will just have to lump it. All right, off you go."

But when Harding had gone to the radio room, O'Rourke's grin vanished to be replaced by a look of bewilderment. What, he asked himself, had the German E-boats been doing off the mouth of the Humber? The convoys which had used to sail from Hull to Russia had ceased. Indeed very little shipping left the Yorkshire port these days and what did was usually escorted by destroyers and frigates, which the much smaller E-boats wouldn't dare tackle. What was going on?

But there was no answer to that question. In the end, Lieutenant O'Rourke gave up and concentrated on conning the motor-launch back into the Humber.

Chapter Two

"Great balls of fire," Lt. Commander Keith bellowed, his purple face an angry as ever, a vein ticking furiously at his temple. "What the devil's going on?" He stood on the narrow spit of sand at Spurn Point and stared with the equally curious coastal defence gunners at the wrecked E-boat which now lay stranded on the beach beyond. There were about 20 dead Germans lying sprawled in the wet sand in that curious, abandoned manner of those who had been done to death violently.

Despite the bleak scene, O'Rourke grinned to himself. Howling Mad was glaring at the dead Germans as if he expected one of them to leap to his feet and explain his reason for being there.

"I feel like a bloody virgin wallflower at the local dancehall, keeping my knobbly knees together in case some nasty matelot tries to put his hairy paw up my knickers! Totally out of the scene." Howling Mad's face flushed an even darker purple. "I wish to God's name that someone would tell me what the bloody Huns were up to!"

O'Rourke cleared his throat discreetly and said, "Sir, we've just had a signal from their Lordships. They're sending someone from Naval Intelligence up on the noon train from King's Cross. He's going to look into the matter more closely."

Howling Mad looked at the young officer as if he had just vomited down the front of his duffle coat. "Naval Intelligence," he sneered. "Bloody lot of pansies and nervous nellies. Oh, come on young O'Rourke, let's go and have a look-see." Impatiently, Howling Mad pushed through the gaping coastal artillerymen and ignoring the sign stating 'Danger-Mines', scrambled down to the shingle.

Together the two naval officers wandered from one dead German sailor to the next, noting that several of them had been badly burned. "Look like a lot of blacks," Howling Mad said unfeelingly, but O'Rourke told himself that the flotilla commander had been fighting the Germans when he had still been at school. Howling Mad had seen a lot of fighting over the past five years. He had become hardened to death.

The minutes passed, the only sound the sad calls of the gulls and the crunch of shoes on the shingle. Leaving Howling Mad to stride on, making his ghastly inspection of the dead, O'Rourke wandered closer to the beached E-boat, her sides blistered and scarred by the fire from her engine-room which looked like the symptoms of some loathsome skin disease. Suddenly he spotted it. A square of some kind of bakelite material with a thick pencil attached to it by wire. He frowned at the strange-looking device and then, without thinking he picked it up and applied the thick pencil to the square. Ignoring the squeaking the pencil made, he wrote his own name on the board. He frowned, what the devil was the device used for? He couldn't recall ever seeing anything similar in the Royal Navy. But before he could ponder the matter any further, Howling Mad called sharply, "Over here, young O'Rourke. At the double!"

He turned and trotted to where the flotilla commander

was staring down at yet another dead German. At first O'Rourke thought the man had suffered 100 per cent burns, but when he came closer he saw that he was wrong. The man had not suffered any burns at all. Instead his body was encased in a thick rubber suit, with only his face and hands free of the protective material.

Howling Mad flashed his subordinate another one of his angry looks and barked, "Now what's an E-boat doing with a Hun dressed up as a frogman, eh?" He looked almost accusingly at O'Rourke. "Something ruddy fishy about that, isn't there, O'Rourke, what?"

"Yes, I think there is, sir," the other officer agreed somewhat hesitantly. One always had to weight one's words when talking to the flotilla commander.

"Obviously the Hun was going to be sent overboard dressed like that. But why and to do what?" Howling Mad's eyes narrowed. "And what do you make of that leaded line wrapped around his stomach?" He pointed at the thick roll of stout twine, which carried a small weight at regular intervals.

O'Rourke did a quick calculation from what he could see of the twine and said, "As far as I can judge, sir, it's marked off at 2 m intervals. That would be just over 6 ft. Could be used for marking off something or other."

"What?" Howling Mad shot at him.

O'Rourke shrugged a little helplessly. "I can't say, sir."

Howling Mad muttered something under his breath and turned. "Come on. We'll let the Intelligence wallah try to work it out. That's what he's paid for. Probably some bloody university don, who'd get seasick on the Serpentine!"

*   *   *

22

Commander Ian Fleming turned out to be nothing of the sort. Tall, languid, with a long face and broken nose, he was the typical old Etonian who would obviously never let anyone fluster him, even Howling Mad Keith. He waited till the leading Wren who had brought them their tea was outside again and said, "Well bred and pretty legs. Always like my gals like that. You're a lucky chap, Keith!"

Howling Mad glared at him, but Fleming of Naval Intelligence didn't seem to notice. Carefully he took a sip of his tea, then brought out a gold cigarette case, took out a hand-rolled cigarette, obviously expensively made somewhere in Bond Street, lit it and then placed the cigarette in an ivory cigarette holder to puff out the smoke with a contented sigh.

Sitting behind Howling Mad, O'Rourke allowed himself a smile. This Intelligence man from the Admiralty's Room 39, home of Naval Intelligence, was something of a card. Outside, a party of ratings were marching briskly down Hull's Hedon Road to the docks, singing lustily. *"This is number one and I've got her on the run. Roll me over in the clover and do it again. Roll me over in the clover . . .!"*

It was too much for Howling Mad, who obviously was already fuming at the behaviour of the languid officer from the 'Wavy Navy', as he had referred contemptuously to the Hostilities only officer, from the Royal Navy Reserve, who wore wavy stripes of rank. He rushed across the room, flung open the window and bellowed to the Petty Officer in charge of the ratings, "Stop that bloody indecent caterwauling at once!"

The Petty Officer turned ashen. Everyone feared Lt. Commander Keith. "Ay, ay, sir," he stuttered, so shocked

that he even forgot to salute. "At once . . . at once . . ."
The singing died away.

Howling Mad grunted and slammed the window.
"Well, Commander?" he demanded to Fleming. "What
did you find out?"

Fleming took the ivory holder out of the side of his
mouth slowly, very slowly, and countered with a question
of his own. "Ever heard of a naval unit called COPP?"

"Never," Howling Mad snorted. "What's that when
it's at home?"

Keith's violent manner didn't seem to worry Fleming
one bit. "Those are initials for the Royal Navy's Com-
bined Operations Pilotage Parties," he explained easily.

"So?"

"They are the people who measured up the beaches
in North Africa, then Sicily and finally at Normandy,
preparatory to the invasions of those places."

"Well, what has all this got to do with our Hun
E-boat, pray?" Keith barked. "Commander, you must
realise that I haven't got all the time in the world. We
do more than drink pink gin and tea here, you know,"
he added pointedly.

O'Rourke felt for the elegant man from Naval Intelligence. But Fleming took it all in his stride. "Let me
please explain how a COPP team works."

"If you must," Howling Mad growled grudgingly.

"They are usually dropped by sub," Fleming went on.
"A two-man canoe team. Both men, usually an officer and
an other ranker, are first-class swimmers. Once they reach
their objective, the paddler keeps the canoe in position
while the other chap in the rubber suit goes overboard
and sets about his task."

Despite his normal impatience and hair-trigger temper,
Howling Mad was beginning to show some interest,

as was O'Rourke, who wondered where all this was leading.

"Now the main function of the team," Fleming continued, "apart from noting the enemy's beach defences, is to measure the gradient of the beach and the shallows beyond. This he does by means of a thin fishing line, leaded at every 10 yards."

Howling Mad whistled softly. "You mean like that twine we found on the dead Hun?"

"Exactly, Commander. By moving backwards and then eventually swimming backwards, too, he notes the gradient of the beach and the shallows beyond, taking down the details on a bakelite pad attached to the forearm."

O'Rourke caught his breath and exclaimed, "You mean like the one I found on the beach at Spurn Point?"

Fleming nodded and took out another hand-rolled cigarette from that extravagant gold case of his.

"So you think that the Hun was intended to be landed by the E-boat to measure up the entrance to the estuary?" Howling Mad snapped.

Fleming released a stream of blue smoke carefully and slowly like a man who was doing some hard thinking. "Yes, Commander, I think that is very likely indeed."

"But what for?"

"Well, Commander, the old charts and tables which the Germans would have from before the war are now well out of date. The experts tell me that due to erosion and the tides the shape of the coast in these parts is changing constantly."

Howling Mad nodded his agreement. "Yes, you are right there. *We* who sail these waters," – even now he couldn't avoid the dig that he was a sea-going sailor while Fleming was a London-based office Johnny – "have to be damned careful we don't run aground. The shallows change all the damned time. All the same," he added, "what can the Hun want in the Humber at this stage of the war? This is 1945, *not* 1940."

"Exactly," Fleming agreed, his eyes pensive. "But I think we can agree on this, Commander. The Huns are not going to risk two valuable E-boats for nothing. They are up to something." His voice rose. "With your permission, Commander Keith, I'd like to stay here for another day or so and see if anything else materialises."

Howling Mad shrugged. "Of course. No skin off my nose. We'll put you up at the Station Hotel in Paragon Street. I believe they serve Earl Grey tea there."

Behind the flotilla leader, O'Rourke shook his head. Howling Mad would never let up.

"Jolly good," Fleming said easily. Then he caught even Howling Mad by surprise. "Do you think, Commander, they could supply me with a whore for the night?" He gave Howling Mad a fake smile. "I feel the sap rising. Must be this bracing northern air." He rose, put on his cap, gave a perfunctory salute to no one in particular and left, leaving Howling Mad seated there in open-mouthed amazement.

Chapter Three

Hull's Paragon Street station was full of the hustle and bustle of wartime. Hard-eyed Red-caps, armed with holstered revolvers, watched the platforms for deserters. Self-important Railway Transport Officers with their armbands strode back and forth, ticking off items on their checkboards. Local prostitutes in high heels and rabbit-skin imitation fur coats waited for customers prepared to pay a pound for a quick grope in the shadows. And everywhere there were sailors, pale-faced, with artificial silk scarves round their necks, caps stuck at the backs of their heads (contrary to regulations), lugged their kitbags to and fro.

Fleming, still smoking with his affected ivory cigarette-holder, casually acknowledged their salutes, though he did receive some rather curious looks from some of the hard-faced petty officers – it wasn't every day that you saw a lieutenant-commander, even one of the Naval Reserve, using a cigarette holder – and strolled to the entrance to the fine old Victorian station hotel. Obviously there were plenty of whores in the bombed-out coastal city. Surely he would be able to find one this night who be able to cater for what he called his 'special needs'. He passed through the blacked-out door to the reception desk, oblivious to the curious eyes which followed his progress. He walked to the desk, put down his case and rang the bell. Nothing happened. He grunted. Ian Fleming was used to being attended to immediately. It was something he had learned as a boy at Eton. He rang the bell again. Still nothing happened. He clicked his tongue a little angrily.

Behind him, the man who had been following him since he had arrived at the station, cleared his throat and said, "I think Joe's just got to the lav, sir. He won't be half a sec."

Fleming turned in that slow, languid fashion of his. It was something else he had learned at Eton. Never appear to be in a hurry or flustered. A small man with a lopsided face was beaming at him, his mouth full of cheap false teeth. "You work here?" he demanded.

"In a manner of speaking," the little man said and winked.

Fleming frowned. What did the fellow mean. "How?"

The little man in his cheap blue suit looked to left and right in the gloomy reception hall, as if to ensure he wasn't being heard. "Well, sir," he said when he was satisfied that no one was listening. "Joe and me knows how you naval gents like yer bit o' fun when yer ashore and that you ain't got no time to go out looking. So—"

"You mean you're a procurer?" Fleming interrupted.

The little man with the ugly false teeth looked puzzled. "*Eh?*" he said.

"I mean are you a pimp?" Fleming asked haughtily.

"I wouldn't put it like that, sir," the little man whined. "Just like to help an officer and gent out, who's risking his life for the old Mother Country."

"For a consideration?"

The little man grinned. "Yer can't get nowt fer nowt, as they say up here, sir," he answered cheerfully.

"All right," Fleming said. "What I'm looking for is – a little special?"

The little man's look brightened even more. "You mean French kissing and – er," he lowered his voice even more, "that other stuff?"

Fleming shook his head. "Not that at all. I'd like a girl who doesn't object to – er – rough stuff, if you follow me?"

"Exactly, sir, *exactly*! Cost a bit, though. There's plenty o' trade in Hull, yer know. The lasses are doing all right!"

"Can you fix me up or can't you?" Fleming demanded. He hated dealing with such people, but it was a case of necessity. In London he had several society friends who would cater for his 'special needs' quite voluntarily, and for nothing.

The little man gave him a cunning look, as if trying to assess him. "It won't be easy, sir, but I think I could do it for a consideration. The lady's gonna cost yer a big white one—" he meant a £5 note – "that's for the whole night," he added hastily, "and there'll be a quid in it for me. Yer'll have to give Joe ten bob to get 'er in. The management here in the Station Hotel is very finicky. So that'll be—"

"All right, all right," Fleming interrupted him impatiently. "I'll pay this Joe of yours the lot. Is that all right with you?"

"Smashing, sir!" the little man answered with alacrity. "When would you like her?"

Fleming looked at his Rolex, solid gold naturally, and answered, "Give me a chance to grab a bite to eat and have a few grogs first. Let us say the witching hour shall be nine o'clock."

"Righto, sir. Just one thing, sir."

"Yes," Fleming said and hit the bell once again. From somewhere in the office behind reception came the sound of shuffling, ancient feet.

"Could I have yer name?"

Fleming hesitated, then he answered. "Lieutenant Commander Ian Fleming."

"Thank you, sir. Joe'll know where to bring her then. She's a strapping lass. She can take her punishment, never fear." The little man in the shiny blue suit winked and then he was gone, disappearing as mysteriously as he had appeared. Fleming frowned then dismissed the pimp from his mind, as he always did with servants. The man had fulfilled his function and he would be paid for it. That's what servants were for, weren't they?

Five minutes later he was trundling upwards in the ancient lift with Joe, the receptionist, all cracking bones and wheezes, saying, "There's some talk, sir, of Winnie" – he meant Prime Minister Winston Churchill – "coming up to 'ull at long last . . ."

It was only afterwards that Fleming registered the full import of that statement.

A hundred yards away, the little pimp waited for the telephone kiosk to be free, shuffling up behind the long line of sailors waiting to talk to home. Then finally it was his turn. First he called the whore, 'Big Rosie', as she was called in his circles. 'Big Rosie' would do everything and anything for money. She had even been rumoured to take on lascars from the boiler-rooms of merchantmen, something that most of the other whores wouldn't do. "If they've got a cock, black, white, red or green," she was wont to boast, "I'll service it, as long as they've got plenty of the readies." He told her what the situation was and she answered, "All right, but if he's gonna knock me about I want double the usual – three quid."

"And you shall have it my old dear," he answered airily. "You deserve it."

When she put the phone down, he called another number: the one they had first given him back in 1941 when he had started working for them. They answered at once, as if they had been waiting for his call all along, as they probably had. "Igor?" he queried.

"*Da*," the answer came.

Swiftly he told them what he knew, which wasn't much save for the latest bit of information he now possessed.

"Say that once again, please," Igor said in his accented but careful English.

The little man in the shiny blue suit told him, "Lieutenant Commander Ian Fleming from London."

"Intelligence?"

"I think so."

There was a pause at the other end in London and the little man could almost feel Igor's brain racing. Finally, just as an impatient sailor with a white kitbag over his shoulder started to rattle the door of the callbox, the Russian said, "Keep on to this man Fleming. If anyone will be in a position to find out how much the English will know, it will be him. *Dosvedanya!*"

"*Dosvedanya*," he repeated the farewell automatically as the line went dead.

He opened the door of the callbox and the impatient sailor snarled, "Don't yer know there's a war on, chum?" and pushed him to one side.

The little man didn't mind. This new assignment from the Russians would mean more money, money to be tucked away nice and safe so that he could bugger off from this rotten country once the war was over. Happily whistling the old ditty about the '*mate at the wheel had a*

31

bloody good feel at the girl I left behind me,' he strolled out into the blacked-out ruins, telling himself things were going very nicely indeed, ta very much.

One hour later Fleming was barking at the big whore. "Now come, let's have those knickers off you – *quick!*" He made a threatening gesture at the blousy blonde. "Or it will be the worse for you, understand?"

"I understand, sir," Big Rosie answered, appearing to be afraid. In fact, she was bored by the whole thing. She had been bored with men for years now, but it was good money and it was better than working in a munitions factory 60 hours a week for £4 10s. She pulled down her art-silk knickers and exposed her plump rump to Fleming, who licked his suddenly dry lips, as he raised his big hand to slap her buttocks.

Outside, Joe, the elderly receptionist, pressed his eye to the keyhole to spy on them, as he had been ordered to by the little man in the blue suit. "Every little bit of info helps, Joe," he had said, slipping the receptionist another 10s note. "The more you can get on people the better," he had winked knowingly, "especially if it's something mucky, and most of them toffs are mucky buggers!"

"Ay," Joe had agreed in that reedy, ancient voice of his. "The things I've seen in this place over the years!"

Now as he squinted through the keyhole, he told himself that the naval officer with the lah-de-dah voice was leaving himself wide-open for the squeeze, the way he was going on with Big Rosie like that, smacking her arse till it was red all over. The little man would be glad to hear that.

That kind of mucky carrying on was always useful for

a bit of blackmail. Down below, the bell of the reception desk sounded.

"Dammit!" the old man cursed to himself. He was going to miss the best bit. Reluctantly he rose and started to creak downstairs.

Inside the bedroom Commander Ian Fleming finished the spanking and in a commanding voice he ordered the girl, "Now, on that bed, young woman, and spread your legs – at once!"

Next moment he had thrown himself upon the fat, blousy whore and was enthusiastically pumping away at her. For her part, she wondered whether he'd be done with her before the fish and chip shops closed. She just fancied a bagful of fish and taties.

Chapter Four

Commander Fleming awoke with a start. Instinctively he reached out a hand to feel if anyone else was in bed with him. But the whore had long gone. Of course. He had really rattled her bones. Women liked being treated rough, even whores. How she had moaned and groaned when he stuck it in her. "More," she had sighed desperately, "give me more . . . Deeper! *Please hurt me!*" He smiled lazily at the memory. Then he was fully wide awake.

Outside, the ack-ack guns were thundering and through the bedroom window (he had always hated the blackout so he had pulled back the blackout curtains before he has fallen into an exhausted sleep) he could see the cherry-red flashes of the AA guns and the icy white lights of the searchlights scouring the clouds with their harsh fingers, looking for the intruder. It was the noise which had awakened him.

He got out of bed and flung on his expensive silk dressing-gown. The lino was cold to his bare feet. That didn't matter, for already his brain was racing electrically. What was the Hun doing raiding Hull at this stage of the war? Nowadays the city was of no strategic importance. Besides, since the summer of 1944 the Hun had always used his V-weapons, the buzz bombs and the rockets, to attack

34

British targets. Why a conventional raid, if that was what it was?

He moved to the window, still criss-crossed with brown paper strips to make it splinter rather than blow out altogether if a bomb fell nearby. He flung it open. The room was flooded with icy air and he shivered. All the same, he craned his neck through and stared at the velvet veil of the night sky.

Somewhere a German plane was dropping what the Germans called 'Christmas Trees': great bundles of flares which came down very slowly and illuminated the area below for nearly half a mile. He sucked his teeth and wished he had brushed them before he had fallen asleep. His mouth tasted of cheap whisky and anything cheap hurt his soul. He watched as the searchlights tried to cone the intruder coming along the Humber and asked himself again what the Huns were up to.

Hull was the most bombed port in Britain. There had been at least 3,000 raids on the place ever since Hull had become the key supply port for Russia back in 1941. The Hun surely had a whole archive of reconnaissance photographs of the area. Why were they attempting to take new ones at this late stage of the great conflict?

Suddenly the myriad searchlights, flashing from the Yorkshire and Lincolnshire sides of the estuary, coned in on the German reconnaissance plane. Fleming recognised the silhouette immediately. It was an old-fashioned twin-engined Junkers 88. Desperately the pilot, probably blinded by the white incandescent light from below, weaved from left to right, attempting to escape from the trap. But the radar-controlled 20mm Bofors homed in on the lone plane and flak started to explode all around the Ju 88. By some miracle the Junkers survived a few more moments. Then its luck ran out.

The port wing was hit. It broke away and fluttered like a metal leaf through that icy light and vanished into the darkness. A parachute blossomed, and another. Yet another. Then the Ju 88, totally out of control, fell out of the sky and with the remaining engine screaming fell to the Humber, trailing smoke and flames behind it.

Suddenly, the searchlights clicked off and Fleming blinked several times in the sudden darkness. Then the flak ceased. From Hedon, farther up the estuary, the sirens began to wail the 'All clear'. The dismal but welcome sound was taken up by other sirens getting ever closer to the city centre. The raid was over.

Slowly, thoughtfully, Fleming closed the window, not even noticing how cold he was, for his mind was too full of this new piece of knowledge. First the E-boat with its pilotage group. Now the reconnaissance plane. What did it mean? Why was the Hun showing so much interest in Hull, 'the arsehole of the world,' as Commander Keith had called it so aptly the day before.

In sudden anger Fleming punched his pillow. He hated not to know what was going on. All his life since his first days at Eton he had wanted to be in control of a situation. That's why he liked to beat women before he made love to them. Then he was in control and not the wench, as they were usually when men were fools and besotted with lust or love. Now he was totally out of control.

Something was going on here at this remote northern port. But what; in God's name? Suddenly he made a decision. He stripped off his dressing-gown washed, and began to put on his uniform, shivering in the cold of the unheated bedroom. If that Hun reconnaissance plane had crashed on land instead of in the estuary he was going to have a look at it. Perhaps it would reveal a clue to what the Huns were up to?

*　　*　　*

"Duty officer," O'Rourke said a little wearily. It was two in the morning. The coke for the little cast-iron stove had given out, it was freezing in the duty officer's room, and he still had four hours before his relief came on.

"Commander Fleming here," the now familiar voice came over the line. "Can you indent for a vehicle, perhaps a staff car, if we're in luck? I want to have a look-see at that Ju they've just shot down. You saw it, I take it?"

"Yes sir, I did. It crash-landed between Hedon and Patrington, so the pongoes report."

"Excellent!" Fleming snapped. "The Huns who parachuted out, got 'em yet?"

"Not yet, Commander," O'Rourke replied. "But the Home Guard have been alerted. They're on the lookout."

Home Guard, the name rang some sort of bell in Fleming's head, but for the moment he didn't know why. So he said, "I'll expect you and the car within 15 minutes." It was not a request but an order.

In spite of his weariness O'Rourke, who had attended a minor public school, St Peter's York, grinned. There was the true voice of Eton, he told himself. "Yessir," he answered, "will be done." The line went dead.

The Junker's battered frame lay in a field just beyond Patrington's fine Gothic church. It had ploughed through the snow for a good 50 yards or more before it had finally come to rest, with the pilot slumped dead across the controls. Middle-aged Home Guardsmen with fixed bayonets plodded around it, being told by the village policemen at periodic intervals to "keep yer thieving paws off'n it. The RAF will want to have a look at it, yer know."

The car came to a stop and as the two officers stepped out into the pre-dawn gloom the policemen and the Home Guardsmen snapped to attention.

Fleming took control immediately. He turned to the NCO in charge of the Home Guard platoon, an elderly man with the sweeping white moustache of an old-time cavalry man, his chest ablaze with medal ribbons, dating back, or so it appeared to O'Rourke, to the Boer War. "Got the ones who baled out?"

"Not yet, sir," the NCO answered in a very fruity accent, which told O'Rourke that the NCO was probably an ex-officer and some kind of local land owner. "But we will. They can't get far in East Yorkshire without being spotted. The terrain's too flat and there are no woods to speak of."

Fleming ignored the comment. "Come on, O'Rourke," he commanded, "let's have a look inside her."

Together they pushed their way through the narrow hatch, crunching over broken screens and metal nostrils filled with the stench of burning and death. Behind the dead pilot the radio operator was crouched over a small desk, a stanchion driven clean through his leather-helmeted head.

Fleming didn't seem to notice. He said, "See if we can find their maps. They might give us some sort of clue as to what their mission was."

"Yes sir," O'Rourke said and tried to avoid looking at the dead radio operator with that terrible metal protruding out of the back of his head.

For a few minutes they worked their way through the jumble of the crashed *Luftwaffe* aircraft, while outside one of the Home Guards was saying in the flat, broad accent of East Yorkshire, "Ay, it's gonna be a lot of bullshit, you can say that agen. The CO's put in for a special supply o' Blanco and Brasso. They say we're gonna have a company commander's inspection, then a battalion commander's and after that, would you believe it, a brigade commander's as well. Blind 'em with bullshit, that's what I think, Charlie."

"Ay," his mate agreed. "But it's not every day that his nibs comes all the way from London . . . besides this is gonna be the last parade, Alf. We'll get another medal and that'll be that."

Fleming unconsciously registered the conversation between the two middle-aged civilian soldiers, but thought nothing of it. He concentrated on finding the pilot's map or flight plans. But when he did he was disappointed. As he called to O'Rourke, searching the back of the plane, "Nothing. Just routine stuff. Seen the same sort of stuff in wrecked Hun planes a dozen times—" Fleming stopped short, realising that the younger officer wasn't listening. "Anything?" he asked hopefully.

O'Rourke straightened up, his handsome young face set in a puzzled frown. "Well, I don't know exactly, sir," he said hesitantly. He held up the charred piece of paper he had just found. "This bit's in English, sir."

Fleming reacted immediately. "Bring it over, O'Rourke," he commanded and flashed his torch so that the other officer could make his way faster through the jumbled confusion that was the crashed reconnaissance plane's wrecked interior.

Crouched next to the dead radio operator, they stared intently at the charred piece of paper which O'Rourke had just found. It was a tattered page from what appeared to be an English newspaper. "'*Scarborough Mer—*'" Fleming read aloud. "*Mer* . . . that'll stand perhaps for *Mercury*. And look at the date . . . October 1914 . . . And there you can just make out some sort of headline."

He peered more intently at the charred piece of paper. "'*Terrible atro . . . German High Sea Fleet bomb . . .*' There it ends." He bit his bottom lip in frustration. "What the hell does it mean?" He made his mind up swiftly. "Come on outside. We'll ask that NCO. He looks old enough to remember 1914."

Hurriedly they scrambled out of the plane and dropped into the ankle-deep snow. "Sergeant," Fleming called. "We seem to have found a copy of an old paper, something called perhaps the *Scarborough Mercury*."

"Still exists, sir," the plummy-voiced Home Guard NCO answered. "Been published since last century."

Fleming, too excited to be interested in the local paper's history, snapped, "Now then can you perhaps recall if anything special happened in Scarborough in 1914?"

"Yes, I can," the NCO answered without hesitation. "I had just joined the East Riding Yeomanry as a subaltern that autumn when we heard about it. It went through the barracks like wildfire. After all quite a few of the troopers came from Scarborough and area. Farmers' sons and labourers—"

"What happened?" Fleming cut in impatiently.

"The German High Seas Fleet suddenly appeared off the north-east coast between West Hartlepool and Scarborough and began bombarding several coastal resorts, Scarborough in particular."

"They did *what*?"

The old ex-cavalryman repeated his statement, adding, "It was a terrible blow to British pride. The Germans had fooled the Home Fleet and people asked at the time what the Royal Navy was up to, letting the Hun get out and into the North Sea like that. Terrible stink." The NCO shook his grizzled head at the memory.

Fleming stared at O'Rourke in the dawn greyness and

asked in a shaky voice, "Why does a Hun recce plane carry with it an old local paper published over 30 years ago, O'Rourke? Eh?"

But O'Rourke had no answer to that overwhelming question.

Chapter Five

Four hundred miles away that same dawn, the new crew had been mustered, well over 1,000 men, all volunteers, and for the most part hardened U-boat crews who no longer had any U-boats in which to attack the hated English enemy.

"*Still gestanden!*" the command echoed and re-echoed around the barracks square at Murwik, as 1,000 pairs of boots clicked and the men, the blue ribbons of their caps flying in the morning wind, slammed rigidly to attention.

On the hastily erected little stage, the senior officer turned and flung Grand Admiral Doenitz, the head of the German Navy, a tremendous salute. "*Melde gehorsam ein hundert Offiziers and ein Tausend Mann, Herr Grossadmiral!*" he barked the accepted formula at the thin-faced Admiral with his keen, hard-blue eyes opposite him.

Doenitz touched his grey gloved hand to his cap and rasped, "*Danke, Herr Kapitan.*" Doenitz turned and faced the assembled crew, studying their tense faces for a moment, as if he wished to etch their features on his mind's eye for ever.

Down below the duty crew watched the 'Big Lion', as he was called by his 'blue boys', just as keenly. They had come from every naval base along the Baltic, lured by the promise of extra rations and 'a cause vital to Folk, Fatherland and Führer', as the official message had stated. All of them knew that it might entail the final sacrifice, but all the ex-U-boat crews knew as well that most U-boat men never survived more than a couple of patrols. They had been prepared to die for the Fatherland right from the start.

Doenitz cleared his throat and stepped closer to the microphone. "Officers . . . men of the German Navy . . . comrades," he rasped into the microphone. In the skeletal trees around the barracks square, the rooks rose into the grey winter sky, cawing in hoarse protest. "Stand at ease!"

Gratefully the sailors, who had been waiting in the freezing wind for an hour for the 'Big Lion' to arrive, relaxed a little.

"I will not waste words," Doenitz went on. "All of you know that this is the eleventh hour for our poor hard-pressed Fatherland. The enemy is at the gates both to East and West. Both are poised to cross our frontiers and attempt to level the death blow at the 1000-year Reich which our beloved Führer, Adolf Hitler" – he barked the name as if it were in italics – "has created."

He wagged a gloved finger at them. "But this will *not* happen," he continued. "For you, my brave chaps, are going on a mission which will undoubtedly break up the dastardly enemy coalition against the Fatherland." He paused and once more looked around at their keen young faces, reddened by the wind. "Some of you might not come back from this mission. No matter. You will die in the knowledge that you will have become immortal, your names written into the pages of our glorious history, names that school-children will learn in centuries to come. You will leave here soon for your destination. When you return you will do so as heroes." He turned and looked at *Kapitan zur See* Hartmann, who would command the new crew.

The burly ex-U-boat skipper understood the look. He raised his cap and yelled without the aid of the microphone, "*Dreimal hoch fur den Herrn Grossadmiral!*"

As one a thousand young voices gave the thin-faced head of the Navy three cheers. Doenitz allowed himself a cold smile of pleasure and then he called in high good humour, "Well, boys, it's not often that you get drilled by a Grand Admiral!"

The men grinned and Doenitz snapped, "Parade will come to attention."

A thousand pairs of heels clicked together.

"Officers will stand their detachments down for 12 hours. There will be schnaps – and girls – for those who want them."

Someone yelled, "Thank you, Grand Admiral!"

Again Doenitz allowed himself a thin smile and then went on to order, "Officers will attend me in 15 minutes. Men will dismiss – *dismiss!*"

Smartly the sailors broke ranks, hurrying off to the various barracks where they knew the Admiral would have had plentiful supplies of drink supplied. Then they would be off to the Navy brothels. The officers strolled away more casually, knowing there'd be no booze or beaver for them this day. There was something big, very big, in the wind. They would have to keep their heads clear.

A quarter of an hour later Doenitz faced the assembled officers in the barracks' gym. Outside the locked doors of the gymnasium, sentries stamped back and forth on the gravel paths. Up above three fighters circled the barracks area; it was obvious even to the dullest of the officers present that security was of the highest.

Doenitz waited till the officers had seated themselves on the hard wooden chairs and benches, then he snapped, "Let it be understood right from the start that anyone who breathes a word of what I am about to say to you, gentlemen, will be regarded as having committed high treason. *Klar?*"

"*Klar!*" they roared back in unison.

"Good, gentlemen. Thank you, I knew all the time I could rely upon you. After all you are volunteers. Now let me tell what this is all about."

A sudden hushed silence fell over the gym, as those at the back craned their necks to hear Doenitz's announcement. He let them wait for a moment and then he announced: "Gentlemen, we have raised the *Tirpitz*."

There were gasps of surprise. Someone exclaimed, "Great crap on the Christmas Tree . . . the *Tirpitz* up again!"

"Yes. It has been a tremendous job," Doenitz commented. "We've had over 5,000 men, mostly Jewish slave labour working on the project who we can liquidate in due course. But the *Tirpitz* is definitely back on the surface once more. Indeed at this present moment our skilled engineer crews from Kiel and Bremerhaven are working flat out to get her seaworthy once more. You will probably ask why?" He let his rhetorical question sink in for a few moments, while his audience stared at him in eager anticipation.

"I shall tell you," he said, answering his own question. "The Führer in his infinite wisdom had pondered this problem for a long time. How could he bring down the coalition of our enemies just as Frederick the Great of Prussia did in the 18th century? He decided that only one man, the implacable enemy of our Fatherland, must be killed. If he goes the coalition falls apart and Germany will still achieve victory or at least better terms than those which are being offered to us at this moment by that Jew Roosevelt – total and unconditional surrender"

He paused and stared around at his listeners with that piercing blue gaze of his.

"Who is that man?" he asked after a moment.

He let them wait before once again answering his own question: "The man who must be killed is that plutocratic sot, that drunken English aristocrat – *Winston Churchill!*"

Once more his listeners gasped and Doenitz, carried away by his fervour, raised the forefinger of his right hand aloft like his father, the Lutheran priest, might have done when preaching some fire-and-brimstone sermon to his congregation. "Yes, Winston Spencer Churchill! Rid the world of that dreadful man to whom the Führer offered peace back in 1940 but who refused it and thus prolonged this terrible war, and that will be it. Then the Jew Roosevelt and that Red dictator Stalin will start talking to us."

He paused, his skinny chest heaving with the effort of so much impassioned talking, while his listeners chatted excitedly among themselves, discussing the surprising information, wondering aloud how they could bring about the death of the British prime minister in faraway London. For in the four years since Churchill had taken over power in the British capital, not even the *Luftwaffe* had been able to kill him. What could they, as naval officers, do?

Doenitz seemed to be able to read their thoughts, for he said, "You are wondering what you as members of the *Kriegsmarine*," the German Navy, "can do to liquidate that terrible man, our implacable enemy, eh?"

There was a murmur of agreement from his listeners.

"Well, gentlemen, we are in possession of some key information on the movements this coming month of Herr Churchill. At present he is in Greece trying to stop the communists there. Then he goes to Russia to confer with Roosevelt and Stalin." He gave them a wintry smile. "You wonder how Intelligence knows these things! It is very simple. For the past two years, unknown to the enemy, we have been tapping the underwater cable linking America and Britain. Whenever Churchill talks to the Jew Roosevelt, we listen too, so we know of his movements. On Thursday February 22nd Churchill will address the British House of Commons. Thereafter Churchill will take a special train to the northern English port of Hull." He paused, the wintry smile gone. "There, away from the elaborate defences of London, we shall kill Churchill." Doenitz's voice faltered for one second, then he hurried on, his thin face flushed a little as if he didn't want to consider the meaning of what he had just said. "So far," he continued, "we have experienced some technical difficulties in preparing our plan of attack. But they shall be overcome and the attack will be executed. As you will soon learn it is a brave and audacious plan, but we have done it before, successfully, long ago when the Royal Navy was the most powerful in the world. Now in 1945 the Royal Navy has sent most of its fleet, 250 ships, including all her capital ships, to the Pacific to fight with the Americans against the Japanese. The British do not possess one ship in their Home Fleet capable of stopping the *Tirpitz*. Remember that, gentlemen. Our plan *will* and *must* succeed!"

Doenitz clicked to attention, eyes blazing fanatically. His right arm shot up in the German greeting. *"Death to Churchill!"*

Immediately his audience sprang to their feet and thrust out their own right hands in salute. *"Death to Churchill!"* they bellowed in unison.

"SIEG HEIL!"

Chapter Six

Impatiently Fleming waited until the village doctor finished binding the captured *Feldwebel's* damaged arm. An irate local farmer's wife had captured him with the aid of a pitchfork only an hour before when he had tried to escape in the falling snow. "Yon Jerry," the fat woman in her sacking apron had explained to Fleming, "didn't want to come. But I soon feckled him. He was out like a shot when I went for him with the pitchfork."

Standing behind Fleming, O'Rourke had smiled. He, personally, would have come out 'like a shot' if he had been confronted by the big burly woman, whose muscles bulged bigger than those of many a man.

Now, as the snow continued to fall in a solid sheet, the two of them waited in the doctor's surgery until he had finished binding the airman's wounded arm. "All right, Fritz," the former said finally, "You're as good as new again." He patted him on the arm and picked up his little black bag. "Must be off on my rounds. Feel free to use my place. My wife'll see you out when you're finished." And with that he was gone.

Fleming took his time. He had interrogated prisoners before and knew the importance of establishing one's dominance over them right from the start. So he stared down at the pale-faced airman sitting on the hard wooden chair, slapping the doctor's ruler on the palm of his other hand, while the German watched the movement apprehensively, as if he were half afraid that the Englishman might be about to use it on him.

"*Nun Feldwebel Schirmer*," Fleming started.

The airman looked surprised at Fleming's use of his name. He didn't know that while the doctor had been attending to his arm, Fleming had quietly rifled his tunic and had found his name in the paybook it had contained.

"We know everything about you," Fleming continued, looking down his long, broken nose at the airman, still beating the palm of his hand with the wooden ruler. "We know about your service in North Africa, Russia, and of late here in the West. So there is no use lying to us, especially if you want to see your wife and daughter again after the war." These details too, had been obtained from the prisoner's paybook.

"So, just you tell me exactly what your mission was and we'll have you transferred to the nearest prisoner-of-war camp immediately, where you can sit out the rest of the war in peace."

O'Rourke could understand little of Fleming's fluent German, but he could see by the look on the prisoner's face that the man would break easily. Already his bottom lip was trembling like that of a frightened child ready to break down and cry at any moment.

"What was your mission?" Fleming demanded, knowing that he had got the prisoner rattled.

"A reconnaissance flight down the Humber," the German airman replied without hesitation.

"To find out what?"

"Aerial photographs of the central channel of the river."

Fleming translated for O'Rourke's benefit and said, "What do you make of that, O'Rourke?"

"Well, sir, information of that kind would only be of use be if some vessel over a certain displacement would want to use that central channel."

Fleming nodded his understanding and turned to the *Feldwebel* once more.

"Who wanted this information about the central channel?" he snapped.

The airman shrugged. "I don't know exactly," he replied, trying to please, "but I guessed it was for the *Kriegsmarine*."

"The Navy," Fleming echoed and said to O'Rourke, "It doesn't seem likely that the Germans would be trying to penetrate the Humber at this stage of the war. Could they be thinking of using midget subs?"

O'Rourke shook his head. "Doubt it, sir. They could try of course, but I don't think they would be very successful, especially as the mouth of the estuary is guarded by boom ships, nets and the like and Coastal Command flies a regular hourly patrol in that area. Besides, in the end, what is there for them to sink? A few small coastal freighters or barges going up to York and the like. Wouldn't be worth the effort, I should think."

Fleming considered this, while the prisoner waited anxiously, his eyes fixed on Fleming's haughty, arrogant face. Outside, the snow was still coming down thickly.

O'Rourke broke the heavy silence. "What about asking him about that copy of the old *Scarborough Mercury*, sir? You know, the bombardment thing, sir?"

"Good idea," Fleming agreed, with unusual enthusiasm for him. "Might turn up something there."

Hurriedly he asked the *Feldwebel*: "We found traces

of an English newspaper on board your Ju 88. It details an attack on a coastal town near here back in 1914 by the German High Seas Fleet. What do you know about it, man?"

The prisoner looked puzzled for a moment, then his face lightened. "*Hauptmann* Prien brought it with him," he answered.

"*Hauptmann* Prien?" Fleming queried, puzzled.

"The pilot," the German enlightened him.

"And why did your skipper have it with him here?"

The German shrugged expressively then winced when he felt his arm hurting. "I don't know. He didn't tell us."

Fleming thought for moment before asking, "All right, where did he get that cutting?"

The *Feldwebel* thought for a moment. "He had it with him when he came back from Murwik," he said finally.

"Murwik," Fleming translated for O'Rourke's benefit. "That the headquarters of the German Navy in Northern Waters." He puffed out his bottom lip and because he didn't quite know what to do next he took out his gold cigarette case and went through his customary ritual of lighting a cigarette and placing it in that affected ivory holder. He exhaled slowly, the blue smoke curling up about his long face, while the German stared up at him, obviously wondering what was going on.

"Why would he have been given a copy of the *Scarborough Mercury* at the German Navy HQ, sir?" O'Rourke asked.

"An interesting question like so many we have been asking ever since we found that frogman 48 hours ago. Unfortunately, O'Rourke, we have so few damned answers to them." Fleming took another extravagant puff at his cigarette. "Perhaps when we catch the other two who parachuted out of the Junkers, we might learn more, but for the time being we know this. One," he ticked off the first point with his elegant, manicured and polished nails, "the Germans are trying to assess the depth and features of the Humber."

O'Rourke nodded, as the snow beat against the panes of the little window with ever-increasing fury.

"Two, whatever they are up to has perhaps some connection with what happened in Scarborough all those years ago."

"Perhaps they are going to stage a raid, sir. Last year they did so from the Channel Islands. Their garrison there, trapped since the Invasion, actually attacked the coast of France and got away with it because we didn't expect them to pull tricks like that any more."

"Yes, I've heard of that raid. But what purpose did it serve, O'Rourke?" Fleming said. "They scuttled a couple of our coastal freighters, shot up a French coastal town and took a score of prisoners. They tell me they were rewarded, the raiders that is, with the Iron Cross and a spoonful of jam each, rationed out personally to them by the Hun admiral in charge of the Channel Islands." Fleming laughed scornfully. "Not exactly something to win the war, what."

O'Rourke nodded his head. "I suppose you're right, sir," he admitted ruefully.

"No," Fleming snapped. "There's got to be more to it than that, dammit." He picked up the ruler and slammed it against the desk angrily, making the prisoner cringe.

"*Tirpitz*," the German said suddenly.

Fleming shot him a look. "What did you say?"

"*Tirpitz*," he quavered. "*Hauptmann* Prien said something about the *Tirpitz* when he came back from Murwik."

"But the *Tirpitz* was sunk last year," Fleming protested.

"Yes, I know, sir," the *Feldwebel* said desperately, as Fleming raised the ruler again as if to strike him. "But that's what he said. The whole business was something to do with the *Tirpitz*. That's all I know, honestly, sir." He looked from Fleming's face to that of O'Rourke almost pleadingly. "I thought he'd had a few. The *Hauptmann* liked his *Korn*," referring to German grain gin.

Fleming quickly translated the now terrified prisoner's words and said, "I think I believe him, don't you, O'Rourke?"

"Yes sir, I do. The man's obviously frightened out of his skin. Perhaps he thinks we'll use Gestapo methods on him. But it's another piece of the puzzle, sir."

"And what a fucking puzzle it is!" Fleming snorted, losing his Etonian calm for a moment. "What the devil is the connection between the Humber and the *Tirpitz*, which has been sitting on the bottom of a Norwegian fjord since last November?"

"Sir," O'Rourke said a little desperately.

"Yes?" Fleming said, only half-listening as he pondered the problem.

"The only way to find out is to see if the *Tirpitz is* at the bottom of that fjord. I mean that would be a starter. Then perhaps things might," he looked a little doubtful as he said the words, "fall into place. So far, sir, we've just been tapping in the dark and getting, if you'll forgive me, nowhere."

Fleming nodded, staring at the falling snow. "You're right, O'Rourke. It is time we started doing something.

All these questions without answers are getting us no further at all, I agree with you there." Suddenly he was very decisive. "Let's get this Hun taken care of and then back to Hull. We've got to get the celebrated digit out of the orifice. Somehow I feel that what's going to happen will happen soon and that we've no time to lose."

Abruptly, O'Rourke felt the same.

Ten minutes later they were in the back of the staff car, each man wrapped in a cocoon of his own thoughts and fears, as the driver fought the snow.

PART TWO

The Armed Reconnaissance

Chapter One

"'Come back, come back, Jolly Jack Straw,'" Sparks was reading the *Ballad of Jack Overdue* in his flat, East Yorkshire accent, following the poem with his dirty forefinger in a three-day-old copy of the *Daily Mirror*. "'There's ice in the killer sea. Weather at base closes down for the night. And an ash-blonde WAAF is waiting tea—'"

"For Chrissake," his mate 'Flags', the motor-launch's signaller, cut in grumpily, "put a frigging sock in it, willyer, Sparks, what bloody kind o' rubbish do yer call yon stuff?"

Opposite him in his rumpled hammock, a dirty grey blanket pulled up about him, almost to the balaclava which he wore round his head against the freezing cold, Sparks said, "It's a po-em." He wiped the dewdrop off the end of his red nose with a mitten. "It sez so in this here *Daily Mirror*. So it must be. Ain't yer never heard of po-ems?"

"Course I have," Flags snorted. "I won the handwriting prize back in my council school when I was a young 'un. But that ain't no po-em. Po-ems are supposed to rhyme. Like that one in the heads. Yer know— 'It's no use standin' on the seat, the crabs in this place jump six feet.' Now that's real poetry. Anyhow get on with the *Mirror*. I want to see if Jane's got her knicks off agen."

"Well, she ain't," Sparks grumbled. "Only her bra and

yer can't really see her tits. That's why I'm reading this here po-em."

It was now 48 hours since they had sailed from Hull. O'Rourke had set a course for Bear Island and when they were sure that German radar had picked them up and presumably decided they were heading for Murmansk in Russia, O'Rourke had begun to back-track, heading for the Norwegian coast and the fjord where the RAF had sunk the *Tirpitz* the year before. The icy northern waters up to now had been strangely bare of shipping, allied or enemy. In the far distance they had once spotted what they took to be a German seaplane, perhaps on reconnaissance. But it hadn't detected the motor-launch and after a while it had disappeared eastwards heading for its base in Norway.

Now the crew relaxed, with only half the men on duty while the others lounged, slept and tried to keep warm in the freezing temperatures of the north, kept going by constant mugs of steaming-hot cocoa from the galley.

Up on the bridge O'Rourke and CPO Harding, however, were as alert as ever. Once, when the battle of the convoys taking supplies from Hull to Murmansk had been at its height, these waters had teemed with U-boats and enemy aircraft had swept the skies almost hourly. Now that the convoys no longer ran, the sea was apparently empty of Germans. All the same O'Rourke and Harding were taking no chances. As 'Howling Mad' Keith had told them before they had set sail, "If anything fishy is going on up there, you can bet your bottom dollar that old Jerry will be keeping a weather eye open. So watch your back . . . and that's an order!"

Now the two men on the bridge 'watched their backs', as they steamed southwards down the Norwegian coast, the mountains in the interior beyond the coastal strip heavy with the winter's snow. O'Rourke had conned the motor-launch very close to the shore, reasoning that the Germans wouldn't expect an enemy craft to come in that close. So any enemy aircraft out searching for possible trouble would be flying much farther out to sea.

The two men on the bridge never found out exactly when the 'little bastard', as they called it afterwards, joined them. It must have been half an hour at least before CPO Harding said in sudden alarm, "A shad, sir . . . a bleeding shad to port!"

O'Rourke had never been in the convoys to Russia, but he knew the term well enough from other officers. The dreaded 'shad' or 'shadow', was a spotter plane which would follow a convoy well out out of range of its guns while it called up the bombers from Norway. Instantly he whipped up his glasses and focused them on the spot that the old petty officer was indicating. And there it was, a dark shape, clearly outlined against the harsh white winter sky.

"Bloehm and Voss 138," Harding identified the German plane almost immediately, as the alarm bells started to jangle and the gunners, pulling on their helmets and flash gear, started to double to their weapons.

"What's the drill, Chiefie?" O'Rourke asked, for Harding had sailed in these arctic waters for two years between 1941 and 1943 when the Germans had thrown whole air fleets against the convoys taking supplies to Russia.

"Well, I suggest we don't open up just yet. We'd just be wasting ammo. The cunning bugger knows well enough how to keep out of range. We'll wait till they attack."

O'Rourke nodded his understanding.

"My guess is," Harding went on, "that they'll have drawn most of their aircraft out of Norway. They need all they can get in Germany itself. But they'll have some, you can bet your bottom dollar on that," he added grimly. "Ay, they'll come looking for us all right!"

59

O'Rourke made a snap decision. "Let's make for the coast. It might give us a bit of protection. Those mountains over there will make it more difficult for an attacker."

"That they will, sir."

"Within two hours we could be inside the fjord where the *Tirpitz* sank and by then the light will have gone."

"Yes sir. That's the best way." Harding grinned and showed his yellow teeth. "Perhaps we ought to say a prayer as well."

The minutes passed leadenly while the on-duty watch and the gunners stared at that tiny lone plane droning round and round the motor-launch as if taunting them to start wasting their ammunition on it. Every so often they flashed a quick, apprehensive glance at the land, the direction from which the dive bombers would come. But the sky over the mountains remained bare and empty. If the Germans were being scrambled, and O'Rourke guessed they were, they were coming from a long way off and that would mean their time over the target would be limited. It was one consolation, he told himself.

At two that afternoon, just as the cook appeared, slopping two mugs of steaming cocoa over his tray as he bore the drinks up the ladder to the bridge, they came. "Aircraft off port bow!" the lookout sang out urgently.

The two officers flung up their glasses and the cook, disturbed by the sudden alert, slopped even more cocoa on his tray, muttering as he did so, "Frigging Jerries . . . spoil even a good cup o' cocoa!"

"Stukas," O'Rourke announced, as the first plane slid into the bright circle of calibrated glass. The old-fashioned dive bomber with its fixed undercarriage and gull-like wings was easily identifiable.

"Thank God for that!" Harding next to him breathed. "They're slow. We can tackle 'em. I thought it might be Focke-Wulfs."

Down below, watching the Germans approach, Sparks said to Flags, "Did yer hear the one about the RAF bloke who was up before the King to get a gong. And the King said, 'I heard you shot down a Focke-Wulf to get this.' And the RAF bloke sez, 'No sir, I shot down *two* Focke-Wulfs.' So the King replies, 'Never mind, you're only gonna get one f-f-fucking medal.' The King stutters yer see." He tossed the end of his Woodbine into the sea and adjusted his helmet. "Here they come, Flags!"

For what seemed a long while the three planes seemed to hover in mid-air above the launch like metal hawks. Then suddenly the first one dropped out of the sky, its wing-mounted sirens shrieking with a banshee-like howl. The Stuka seemed to be hurtling towards its own destruction, coming down steeply at an enormous rate as the guns barked, filling the sky with lethal puffballs.

In the very last instant, when it seemed the dive-bomber must crash into the sea, the pilot pulled it out of the dive. Two bombs tumbled from beneath the Stuka's gull-wings, then the launch shook and jerked violently as the sea all about heaved, great gouts of water shooting up in a wild white fury.

On the monkey island behind the bridge, the rating manning the twin Vickers-guns rattled away. Metal spun from the Stuka as it zipped across the surface of the sea, preparing to climb back up. That wasn't to be. Desperately the pilot fought to retain control as flames started to lick the length of the fuselage. In vain. Abruptly the plane's nose dropped. Before the pilot could do anything the Stuka had plunged into the water and sank.

But as wild, excited cheering broke out on the motor-launch, which was now zig-zagging wildly to left and right as it headed at full speed for the partial shelter of the coast, the second came plummeting from the sky. Again the gunners opened up their barrage. Still the German pilot pressed home his attack. Bravely, he continued his dive, missing destruction by inches time and time again.

At the very last moment when it looked as if the German must smash into the sea, the pilot pulled out of his tremendous, death-defying dive. Bombs tumbled from the Stuka. This time the second pilot was more accurate. The motor-launch reeled and heeled under the impact. Shrapnel sliced lethally across the deck. A man's scream was cut short and then his severed head was rolling into the scuppers, trailing blood on the deck behind it like a football abandoned by a careless schoolboy. The radio aerial came tumbling down and angry blue sparks ran down the side of the hull as it fell overboard. Then the Stuka was gone, winging its way swiftly over to the mountains, leaving behind chaos and the gunner on the monkey island slumped dead over his twin Vickers-guns.

Now it became a race between the motor-launch trying to get to the shelter of the coast and the last Stuka which again hovered over the damaged ship, ready for the kill. Desperately O'Rourke flung the craft from side to side to confuse the pilot's aim. Then the dive-bomber was falling out of the sky, siren shrieking, determined to blow the English out of the water for good.

Up on the debris-littered deck, deafened by the roar of the Stuka's engine and the sirens, Flags crossed himself, took off his helmet to cover his genitals just in case and intoned not for the first time, "For what we are now about to receive, may the Good Lord make us truly grateful!"

Chapter Two

Commander Fleming was both excited and puzzled. He was excited because earlier that day he had purchased a dog-whip which Big Rosie had agreed to allow him to use on her for 'two big white ones'. It was a lot of money, but it was worth it, he felt, for the experience. He had never yet used a whip on a woman.

He was puzzled on two counts. Only half an hour before, he had spoken with Commander Keith about the O'Rourke reconnaissance mission to Norway only to be told, "Nothing. O'Rourke agreed to break radio silence once he reached the Norwegian coast. But we've been waiting for six hours now – by this time he should have reached the coast – and there's nothing. We've sent out emergency signals, but again nothing. It's almost as if young O'Rourke has vanished from the face of the earth."

Now, as his staff car was driven through the centre of war-torn Hull, with bombed-out buildings on both sides, Fleming was puzzled again by the activity going on everywhere. There were armies of middle-aged men, obviously employed by the council, busy clearing the snow and although it was going to snow again during the night, they were painting lines on both sides of the roads. Others were erecting large wooden hoardings, of the kind used by advertisers for their posters, to cover the naked fronts of the ruins. Here and there women polished the brass plates of the surviving offices. Once, he queried the naval driver, who had a half-smoked Woodbine tucked behind his right ear below his cap, what was going on, but he didn't know either. "Can't say, Commander. Perhaps some big-wig coming or the like." Then he added with a smirk, "They don't tell the likes of us much, sir."

"Bloody Bolshy," Fleming told himself, "the whole bloody country is going bolshy! If Churchill doesn't look out, they'll elect a bloody Labour government in the next election." Then he sat back in the hard seat of the Humber and thought about the prospects of the night.

Big Rosie was a willing horse. But, of course, he couldn't knock her about too much. She'd make some noise and that would be fatal. Hickson, the bloody hotel manager who had his long, pinched nose into everything, would be on to it like a shot and then all hell would be let loose. Still, the thought of tanning those big, dimpled buttocks excited him greatly and already he could feel the faint stirrings of lust in his loins.

For a while he allowed his thoughts to wander, dwelling on the things he could do to her and make her do for him. Then, against his will, his mind returned to the problem of O'Rourke. He had hoped that O'Rourke might be able to solve the great mystery, but obviously the handsome young skipper had run into some trouble or another. The mine-fields off the Norwegian coast weren't properly charted. The Germans still presumably expected the occupied country to be invaded and they were always mining and re-mining the waters there. O'Rourke's motor-launch wouldn't be the first craft to disappear over there without trace.

So what was he to do?

Should he try to get Coastal Command to send over a Sunderland to do an aerial reconnaissance? But the fjords were exceedingly deep and even ships as big as the *Tirpitz* could disappear into those depths without trace. What was needed was a visual reconnaissance, looking for oil slicks or pieces of wreckage on the surface. That was really the only way to find out what had happened.

Fleming sniffled. As the car approached Paragon Street station he could see that workmen were building some kind of saluting base in the forecourt just in front of the entrance next to the bus station. He registered the fact, but his brain didn't try to explain why; he was too concerned with what had happened to O'Rourke and his motor-launch.

The driver braked and stopped and Fleming got out. As if he had been waiting for him all the time, the little man with the cunning eyes, in the blue suit, sidled out of the shadows. "She'll be here in two hours, sir," he whispered out of the side of his mouth, as if he were afraid that someone might hear. "She's gonna spend the night tonight, so you'll have grease old Joe to get her out in the morning, discreet like. He's on night duty."

Fleming looked down his nose at the little man with disdain. The fellow, he told himself, was beyond all measure. But he needed his services as long as he remained in this remote, hellish place. So he said, "It will be done. You've told her it'll be – er – a bit more painful tonight?"

"Yes sir," the little man answered promptly. "All done and dusted. She's ready to take all yer can give her." He winked knowingly and held out his hand.

Reluctantly, Fleming reached for his wallet and took out the two white £5 notes he had promised, but added another one for the little man.

65

He accepted them with "Ta guvnor. I hope you'll have a nice time, but don't do anything I wouldn't." He appeared to be going, but suddenly stopped short, as if he had remembered something. "I ain't seen that nice young Mr O'Rourke of late," he said, eyes suddenly cunning. "Hope he ain't gone and got hissen in trouble."

Fleming looked at him in that Etonian manner of his, which never noted anything about the lower classes, and failed to see the look in the little man's eyes. "He's at sea," he said curtly.

"Yer," the little man commented with apparent casualness, "I thought I heard that one of the flotilla was heading for Arctic waters. One of the lads at the docks said they was giving out Arctic clobber."

"One of the lads at the docks," Fleming said heavily, "ought to keep his big mouth shut or he might find himself in serious trouble. That's careless talk, you know."

"Sorry sir. Didn't think of it like that, sir," the little man said hastily. "But there's allus an awful lot of gossip among yer dockers."

Fleming ignored the apology. "See that she's here on time, will you," he snapped and then passed into the entrance of the Station Hotel.

The little man watched him go, muttering under his breath, "Toffee-nosed bastard with his frigging cut-glass accent!" He promised himself it wouldn't be long now before he slung his hook to Canada or somewhere like that and then he'd be shot of the lah-de-dah bastards with their public schools for frigging good. Then he thought of the business at hand and as he walked slowly back to the station to see if there was any whisky left at the station buffet, he began to work out what he would tell the Igor.

Obviously, the little man pondered, O'Rourke, who

had been at that bastard Fleming's beck-and-call since he had arrived in Hull, had been sent on some mission connected with what Fleming was trying to find out. That was certain. He knew from his informants at the docks that O'Rourke's crew had been fitted out with Arctic gear, extra thick duffle coats, thick woollen stockings and the like, so obviously they were heading for Arctic waters. But where? It couldn't be Russia. The convoys to Murmansk were long finished. Iceland? He considered that prospect for a few moments as he threaded his way through the throng of sailors and whores. No, most of the British troops up there had been pulled out a year or more ago. So what was left?

He pushed through the swing doors of the wet buffet, coughing suddenly in the thick fug, composed of cigarette smoke, wet clothing and unwashed bodies, and fought his way to the bar, which was already awash with spilled beer. He winked at the woman who ran it and gave her a fake smile, the sour-faced cow with her buck teeth and red nose. "You're looking very glamorous tonight, Dolly. Any scotch?"

She bent forward deliberately so that he could see down her raddled cleavage and filled a glass of precious whisky under the counter. "Two and a tanner," she said, pushing it towards him and gave him the benefit of her buck-toothed smile. Christ! he told himself. She'll be expecting me to fuck her next for a drop of scotch. But he smiled in return and pushed the half-crown in her direction. "Ta, beautiful," he said. "See you later."

She simpered and he pushed his way back through the crowd to a settle at the back of the place. There, he started to consider the problem once more. Suddenly he had it. "Norway!" he said aloud.

Sitting next to him, half dozing on the settle, a sailor

shook his head and exclaimed, "What did yer say, mate? . . . Norway?"

The little man in the blue suit took a careful sip of his precious whisky, which the buck-teethed cow hoarded as if her life depended upon it, and said, "Must have been thinking aloud."

The sleepy sailor looked longingly at the whisky and said, "Some people must have friends in high places, mate."

"Fancy half a pint?" the little man asked on sudden impulse.

"You betcha!" the sailor said. "My mouth feels like a gorilla's armpit!"

The little man fought his way through the noisy throng and brought back the half pint of weak wartime bitter.

"Here's to yer very good health," smiled the sailor. "You're a real gent!" Next instant he had downed half the glass, belched, wiped his lips with his sleeve and said, "Nice bit o' wallop that! Norway? I was down at Gosport in '43 when our midget subs went up there."

"To do what?"

"To sink the *Tirpitz* of course. But they didn't pull it off, as the actress said to the bishop. In the end the Brylcreem boys" – he meant the RAF – "did it. They sank her with their bombers last year. November I think." He picked up his glass. "Down the hatch, mate!"

"Down the hatch," the little man echoed and raised his own glass in the toast, his mind racing electrically now. He thought he had it. It was all something to with this Jerry battleship, the *Tirpitz*. What exactly he didn't know, but that didn't matter. He'd leave that for the Ruskies to figure out. But he had something he could sell them again.

Minutes later he was in the nearest phone box, calling

that secret number in London. As always Igor, his contact, answered. Swiftly he told the Russian what he thought he knew, ending with, "It's all something to do with a ship that the RAF sank in Norway last year."

He could almost feel the tension at the other end of the line 200-odd miles away as he said the words. For a moment or two, Igor remained silent before saying, "Did you say a ship sunk in Norway?"

"That's right. The *Tirpitz*," he answered, knowing instinctively that he was on to something, perhaps a real money-spinner.

Again there was a long, significant pause at the other end till Igor said harshly, iron in his voice, "Never say another word about this. Just do as you are ordered – or else!" The phone went dead and the little man's good mood vanished immediately. He felt a cold finger of fear trace its way down his spine. Slowly, thoughtfully, he walked out of the booth into the cold night.

Chapter Three

It was night. The third Stuka had vanished long ago after trying in vain to knock the motor-launch out with the last of its bombs. The mountains had done the trick. Their close proximity had made the approach run so difficult for the pilot that he had jettisoned his remaining bombs and departed for his base.

Now the stricken craft limped along the coast, trying to find the entrance to the fjord where the *Tirpitz* had gone to the bottom, while the men tried repair the damage as best they could. But as Sparks had told O'Rourke an hour before, "Don't think I can do much with the radio for the time being. We'll just have to stay out of contact till first light, sir. Then I'll try to rig up a makeshift aerial and send a signal then."

O'Rourke nodded his understanding and had concentrated on two things: getting the crew a rough-and-ready meal of corned beef stew and bread and getting as far away as possible from the spot where the last Stuka had attempted to finish them off. As he had said to Harding, "I'm sure they'll report our presence to their authorities and if they've got any surface craft in this area they'll be on their way in due course."

"Ay, you're surely right there, sir," Harding had agreed. "It's gonna be tricky to navigate in these shallow waters in the darkness, but it's the only way."

O'Rourke stood on the bridge, conning the damaged craft, pausing every now and again to dip a hunk of National Loaf in the rapidly cooling mess-tin of corned beef stew, and he realised that the old CPO had been right. The coast of this part of Norway was very rugged, with rocky crags jutting unexpectedly out to sea and with here and there sudden shingle beaches where a ship could easily run aground. But at the same time, he knew that if navigation was difficult for him, any German craft would have the same problems.

Harding came back on the watch just after six and, though he felt absolutely exhausted, O'Rourke didn't leave the bridge. Instead, while the old CPO conned the ship, he concentrated on the charts beneath the shaded light and tried to work out how long it would take them to reach Altenfjord. It was here, at the back of the fjord, three months before, that the RAF had sent the *Tirpitz* to the bottom.

While he worked out the details, Harding called over his shoulder, "How far up the fjord was the *Tirpitz* when she was sunk, sir?"

"About five miles or thereabout," O'Rourke replied. "Why do you ask?"

"Well, my rough guess is that we won't reach the mouth of the fjord till first light."

"That's my guess, too. Go on."

"Well, sir, once we're in the fjord with only one exit, we're right up the creek without a paddle, if a Jerry turns up at the exit."

"Yes," O'Rourke called across. "That's what I've been thinking, too. It's a bit worrying."

"Could I make a suggestion then, sir?"

"Suggest away, Chiefie."

"Why run the risk? If we could lie low close to the coast we wouldn't have to risk the ship."

"But how could we find out about the *Tirpitz*?" O'Rourke asked puzzled.

"We could send a landing party to have a shufti. A ten-mile round-trip shouldn't take more than three hours. I was up in these fjords back in '40 when we attacked Narvik and all of them have got a rough-and-ready road or track running parallel with the water, below the mountains, so it wouldn't be that tough."

O'Rourke absorbed the information for a moment and looked down at the chart. "Yes, you're right. There is a road running up the side of the fjord to some kind of fishing hamlet, I suppose. Yes, that might be it, a small recce party, while the ship lies up at the entrance to the fjord." He made his decision. "I shall take it. You'll be in charge of the motor-launch. If there's any kind of trouble do a bunk. Get that, Chiefie? We'll look after ourselves."

CPO Harding opened his mouth to protest, but thought better of it. The job needed a young, fit man and he was neither. He remembered how, just before they had sailed from Hull, Annie, his wife of 30 years had helped prepare him for what lay ahead. She had handed him the trick crepe bandages and had said, "Get them around yer knees, Harry Harding, while I fix the Wintergreen plaster."

Grumbling that she was fussing like a mother hen, he had carried out her instructions, winding the thick bandages round his boney, crippled knees, while she picked at the plaster with her work-worn fingers.

"I hope it's proper Wintergreen," he had said, finished bandaging his knees. "There's nothing like a real hot Wintergreen to keep the cold out of a man's back!"

"The chemist said it would burn the bollocks off a bull," she answered, finally succeeding in getting her nail between the plaster and its cover.

His mouth had dropped open stupidly. "Did the chemist say that?" he had queried, amazed at her language.

"Course he didn't, yer daft bugger!" she had replied. "The only one that uses language like that around here is you, Harry Harding."

He had chuckled and said, "All right, slap the bugger on."

He had shivered as she had smoothed the plaster along his skinny back and said, "It's real parky at first. All right, where's me shirt?"

She had shaken her grey head in mock wonder. "What would you do without me?" she had declared, handing him his shirt which had been warming in front of the coal fire.

Then with surprising tenderness for such a hard man, he had folded her into his arms, saying, "I don't know, luv. I don't know!"

The tears had flooded into her faded eyes and abruptly she remembered him as he had once been, the first time she had met him just after the Battle of Jutland back in '16, broad and handsome, with teeth as white as the advertisement for Gibbs toothpaste and his brawny chest ablaze with medal ribbons. It had been love at first sight. Now his chest was sunk, his hair had become grizzly and what he had left of his own teeth were gnarled and yellow. She hugged him to her and whispered, "Now look after yersen, Harry Harding. Don't do nothing daft like. I want yer back yer silly old bugger!"

Now as they chugged through the Arctic night, he remembered those last words of hers and told himself he would be doing something 'daft like' if he attempted to lead the patrol.

Behind him, bent over the charts, O'Rourke worked out the route from what appeared to be a little bay at the edge of the mountains not far from the entrance to the fjord. He'd take a couple of men with him, no more, but they'd be armed just in case, though, he told himself, he didn't expect to encounter any Germans. Why should he? If the *Tirpitz* was at the bottom of the fjord, what purpose would they serve there without a ship to look after?

Suddenly the charts and plans were forgotten as, perhaps half a mile to their front, there was a great burst of brilliant incandescent light. Immediately the sea in the area was illuminated and night was abruptly turned into day.

"They're using flares!" Harding yelled, eyes narrowed to slits against that searing light. He reacted instinctively, whipping the wheel half right and the motor-launch sped towards the shore. It was a very dangerous thing to do and Harding knew it. They could easily run aground on that wild, rocky foreshore. But he knew, too, they had to get under the cover of the mountains before a second flare – and he was sure there was going to be one – burst closer to them.

Now they were creeping into the great shadows cast on the water by the snow-capped mountains. "Both dead slow," Harding ordered the engine-room, speaking in a whisper as if whoever had fired the flare might hear him.

The launch slowed down, moving at a snail's pace as the second flare exploded closer this time, seeming to hang in the sky for ever, illuminating everything around him. O'Rourke felt himself sweating despite the cold. *Wouldn't the damned thing ever go out?*

Another flare shot into the sky. This time they saw who had fired it. To their starboard the dark shape of a motor torpedo-boat was outlined, stark black against the glaring white light, and there was no mistaking that knifelike prow and sleek lines. "*S-class MTB,*" O'Rourke hissed, the 'S' standing for *Schnellboot* – 'fast boat'.

Harding ordered both engines to stop so that the noise wouldn't give then away. "Ay, yon'un is a Jerry all right," the ancient CPO agreed grimly. "And the bugger's looking for us, you can be sure of that."

They drifted silently in the lee of the mountains. On the deck the on-duty crew tensed in apprehensive silence. No one spoke. Everyone concentrated his attention on the German craft, which might now have been some half a mile away. All of them knew that on the enemy torpedo-boat other young men like themselves would be searching the shadows for the first sign of them, and that if they were sighted they were trapped between the sea and the land. They were also a good ten knots slower than the more modern German *Schnellboot* MTB and wouldn't be able to raise sufficient speed to make a dash for it and get away into the darkness.

The minutes passed leadenly. Again the Germans fired a flare. Once more the surface of the sea was lit all around and for one long moment, O'Rourke and the crew thought they had been spotted, for the German MTB turned prow forward, as if it were ready to go into action, thus presenting the smallest possible target for any enemy fire.

But nothing happened. Instead of opening fire, suddenly the MTB's engines burst into a great roar. Even in the fresh darkness they could see the great white bone

75

in her teeth as the prow lifted up out of the water and she gathered speed by the instant.

O'Rourke breathed out a sigh of relief. The enemy was abandoning the search in this area.

Next to him, his voice a little strange, Harding said, "I know what you feel, sir. But we're not out of the wood yet. They might well be back tomorrow – this time with spotter planes . . ."

Chapter Four

"Beautiful, ain't it," Sparks said. "Them mountains with the snow and stuff and that water," he indicated the long stretch of the fjord in front of them.

"Bloody parky to my way of thinking!" Flags shivered dramatically, as the two of them trudged through the snow behind O'Rourke. All three of them were carrying rifles, with service revolvers strapped to the canvas belts around their waists.

To both sides there was no sign of life. They might well have been the last men alive on earth; three inferior puny creatures dwarfed by the mountains. "What a place to live!" Flags moaned. "There aren't even any bleeding seagulls!"

Up front, O'Rourke smiled. As long as a matelot grumbled, things were still all right. It was only when he stopped grumbling that there was trouble.

They had left the ship an hour before, well hidden in the little cove with lookouts posted on both sides of the inlet to keep a weather eye open for the return of the German motor torpedo-boat. O'Rourke prayed it wouldn't. Once they had completed their mission, he wanted to get back out to sea as quickly as possible. It was too dangerous sticking close to the coast as they were being force to do.

But if the fjord seemed devoid of human and bird life,

the water itself abounded with fish. In the crystal clear, blue water they could see them everywhere, swimming with silvery grace just below the surface or leaping in great twirling curves like fishy ballerinas. Once they even saw a baby whale trawling lazily through the water, making obscene sounds every time it surfaced to breathe.

It was interesting and broke the boredom of the road march through the snow. So it was that they didn't hear the sounds behind them until it was too late. Then there was a harsh order in a language they didn't understand and they swung round to find themselves confronted by half a dozen men with dark faces and hooked noses, dressed in ragged coats over what looked like blue and white striped pyjamas, and all armed with rifles.

"Cor ferk a duck!" Flags snorted. "Now we've been caught with our knickers down. They've got us, the buggers!"

The tallest of the ragged band let his mouth drop open stupidly when he heard the words. But the look of stupidity was replaced almost immediately by one of absolute, total joy. He lowered his rifle and exclaimed, "You are English? Say that you are English!"

O'Rourke looked at their haggard, worn faces, pinched with cold and undernourishment, and said slowly, wondering who the devil they were, "Yes, as a matter of fact, we are."

The tall man dropped his rifle into the snow. He rushed forward and flung his arms around the astonished young officer, hugging and kissing him, as if he would never stop, crying all the time, the tears rolling down his pinched cheeks, "English . . . *Boshe moi!* . . . English!"

Gently O'Rourke finally pushed him away and asked, "But who are you . . . what are you doing here?"

The ragged man bowed very formally and said, "Professor Anton Levi, formerly the University of Smolensk. Jewish."

Suddenly it dawned on O'Rourke. All these men were Jews – Jewish prisoners of the Germans. "But what are you doing here?" he asked, puzzled, while the others beamed at him and made comments in Russian and Yiddish.

"We work for the *nemetski* – Germans." Professor Levi's dark eyes suddenly glowed angrily at the mention of that hated name.

"Work – doing what?"

Levi said in hesitant English, "We bring ship out of water – big ship! Many of us. Then German, he begin to kill us . . . We run away into mountains. Kill Germans," he added proudly, pointing to the rifle in the snow.

O'Rourke swallowed hard and posed the overwhelming question. "Was the ship the *Tirpitz*?"

"*Da, da!*" Levi answered eagerly. "*Tirpitz* . . . very big ship. *Tirpitz*. Much work!"

Behind O'Rourke, Flags said, "So the jewboys did the job for old Jerry, eh. They raised the frigging *Tirpitz*!"

O'Rourke considered for a moment before asking, "Is the *Tirpitz* here?"

Levi shook his head. *Nyet*," he answered. "Ship go one week now. Then Germans begin killing *Zhid*," he grinned momentarily and translated the Russian word. "Kill Yids."

O'Rourke's brain raced with the startling news. The *Tirpitz* was raised and was presumably underway under her own steam. So there was some connection between the events in Hull and the huge German battleship. What, he couldn't imagine. He'd have to leave that to Fleming and Naval Intelligence. But first he would have to get back

79

to Hull and let them know what he had discovered. He couldn't signal that across the North Sea. The Germans might pick up and de-code the message. He asked one last quick question, "Professor Levi do you know where the *Tirpitz* went?"

Levi looked proud when his title was used. All the same he shook his head and shrugged expressively. "No. One thing."

"Yes?"

"Sailors on *Tirpitz* have no thick clothes . . . like you." He indicated O'Rourke's Arctic gear. He beamed winningly at the young officer. "*Ponemayu* . . . understand?"

O'Rourke did understand. If the crew of the *Tirpitz* were wearing ordinary *Kriegsmarine* uniforms, it was obvious the ship wasn't going to stay in Arctic waters. Behind them, Flags, who had been listening intently to the conversation, exclaimed, "That means the bugger's heading south, sir!"

"Exactly," O'Rourke agreed in the very same moment that the little plane appeared from over the peaks and slowly started to descend. The spotter plane had arrived.

O'Rourke wasted no further time. "Come on, Professor, and bring your chaps with you. We've no time to lose!"

Levi didn't understand all the words but O'Rourke's tone conveyed the urgency of the moment. "*Davoi!*" he called to the others, "*Davoi!*"

At a half-run they started back down the rough road, while the spotter plane came lower and lower.

Two miles away, CPO Harding, who had heard the plane too, made his own quick decision. Bending to the voice tube, he snapped, "Start engines." Then he looked at his watch. He'd give Lieutenant O'Rourke's party another hour. If he was not back he'd move off. He knew it was the same decision O'Rourke would have made. They couldn't risk the ship and the majority of the crew.

Now the gunners tensed at their posts, peering out of the shadows cast by the mountains behind them at that harsh blue winter sky for the first glimpse of the spotter plane. At their posts the lookouts stared out to sea with their binoculars, sweeping their allotted areas at regular intervals to check whether the spotter was accompanied by seaborne craft. But for the time the sea remained empty, an endless rolling mass of green water as far as the horizon.

Time and time again Harding flashed a glimpse at the dial of his wrist-watch, feeling the tension rise inside him as he willed O'Rourke's party to make an appearance over the headline to the right of the motor-launch. But the track remained obstinately empty.

The spotter came over the mountains and began to drone around in lazy circles. From the shadows Harding caught a glitter of glass in the weak winter sunshine. That would be the observer, Harding told himself, sitting next to the pilot and scouring the rugged terrain below with his field-glasses. He felt the man couldn't but help see them. Yet their luck held out. The little single-engined plane continued to circle above them.

Harding flashed another worried glance at his watch. O'Rourke had half an hour to go. Below the deck the engines throbbed urgently as if they were live things, anxious to be moving and underway before it was too late.

Suddenly, startlingly, the plane dived to the right

beyond the headland, its engine note increasing. Harding's heart missed a beat. The observer had spotted something. Was it the O'Rourke party?

Next moment he knew it was. O'Rourke and the two ratings, followed by half a dozen ragged civilians in what appeared to be striped pyjamas, came stumbling and panting into view.

Harding wasted no more time. He nodded to the rating manning the twin Vickers MG on the monkey island behind the bridge. The rating understood immediately. He spun the twin machine-guns round and cocked them, aiming their muzzles in the direction the spotter plane would come from. Squinting through the foresight he waited for it to make its appearance. The shore party were now running all out down the slope which led to where the motor-launch was berthed. Harding swung himself out of the bridge door and yelled, "Ready to cast off!"

The rating at the rope gripped it in readiness, his eyes fixed on the running men. Back on the bridge, Harding poised over the speaking tube. He could feel his heart pounding with the tension. Would they make it before the spotter came over the mountains? He told himself it didn't matter. They'd have to knock the bloody thing out of the sky now. They didn't want its pilot reporting their position back to his base.

The running men were only 20 yards away now. The man at the rope prepared to cast off. Behind his guns the rating took first pressure. Then it was there, racing in at zero feet after the fleeing men. The gunner didn't hesitate. He pressed the trigger. The guns erupted into frenetic life and a vicious hail of white tracer sped towards the surprised plane. At that range and that height, the pilot didn't have a chance. The slugs slammed into his radial engine, tearing it to pieces. Gylcol spurted in a thick white foam, covering the canopy and blinding the pilot. Harding caught one last glimpse of him as he threw up his hands in front of his face in fear. Next moment the plane slammed into the headland, losing both wings and catapulting into the sea. A great splash and it disappeared into the depths of the fjord.

A moment later the exhausted men were clambering aboard, their lungs wheezing like ancient leather bellows. The rating cast off and Harding cried through the voice tube, "Both ahead – slow!"

The motor-launch started to pull away. Beyond lay the empty sea, not a ship in sight. Harding offered a silent prayer of thanks. The spotter plane's pilot had not radioed their position back to his base. They were going to get away with it.

His chest heaving frantically, Lieutenant O'Rourke staggered up the steps to the bridge. Despite the freezing cold, beads of sweat were trickling down his face. With a gesture of his free hand, Harding indicated he should catch his breath before he spoke. But O'Rourke's information was too urgent for that. "Chiefie," he gasped, fighting to control his breathing.

"Sir?" Harding replied, not taking his gaze off the outlet and the sea beyond.

"The *Tirpitz* . . . they've raised her . . . It's gone . . . We've got to get back and report!" Then he leaned against the door, all energy gone, as if someone had opened an invisible tap.

Chapter Five

It was three in the afternoon. The weak winter sun had vanished. The sky above the endless, rolling dark-green sea had become leaden and O'Rourke, recovered and on the bridge once more, guessed they were in for snow. "It's all to the good, Chiefie," he had just stated to Harding as one of the first flurries came down and then ended after a few minutes. "Give us the cover we need."

"Exactly, sir," Harding agreed. "We don't want to be too bloody visible in these water. Too dangerous."

O'Rourke had nodded his understanding and then had concentrated once more on the navigation. In an hour or two it would be dark and then he guessed they would be relatively safe, for by morning he hoped to be in Scottish waters where he would break radio silence and ask for the protection of Coastal Command. For he knew it was vital to get back as quickly as possible – and in one piece – with his startling information.

Perhaps, he told himself, some expert interrogation of the runaway Jewish concentration camp inmates would reveal some clue to where the *Tirpitz* had gone and what her mission was, if, indeed, she had one. As for the prisoners they were down below in the galley wolfing down huge corned beef wads, yelling "*Horoscho!*" ("good") all the time, and washing the sandwiches down with mugs of scaldingly hot cocoa. As the one called Levi had said,

"You English – you live like kings. Such meat!" and he had taken another delighted bite at the stale bread and greasy corned beef.

O'Rourke forgot the Russians. Now it was really beginning to snow and he had to concentrate on the navigation. Visibility was getting worse by the minute.

Next to him, Harding said a little wearily, "I'll be glad when we get back. I'll stay in kip for a solid 24 hours with the old woman warming me feet, I swear I will!"

"You're getting old, Chiefie," O'Rourke humoured.

"Ay, you're right there, sir. I think I am."

"Come off it, Chiefie! You'll go on for ever and a day."

"I doubt it, sir," Harding answered quietly. "I doubt it strongly."

An hour later the snow started to come in from the east. At first it was nothing more than a few lazy flakes, falling gently, softly, almost unnoticed. Gradually, however, the snowfall thickened. On the exposed gun platform the gunners who were now standing-to did physical jerks in their heavy clothing and hob-nailed sea-boots. A couple of would-be comics waltzed together in mock solemnity. But as the snowfall turned into a blizzard their high spirits and physical activity deserted them and they cowered there like beasts in a field, sinking into a brooding, frozen lethargy, as the relentless snow beat against them.

On the bridge, O'Rourke cursed and cursed. Navigation was becoming trickier and trickier. It was an almost total white-out. In the end, although he needed every knot the engines could give if they were to reach Scotland quickly, he ordered the engine-room to slow the revs down. Now everyone was on duty; there was no off-duty watch. Lookout were posted to both sides of the ship, straining their eyes and ears, listening for the slightest sound as they steamed through this white, whirling wilderness.

O'Rourke raged inwardly as he paced the little bridge while Harding took over the conn. The Germans would have radar. They could lock on to him despite the blizzard and he knew instinctively that they would be looking for him now. They would have guessed that he had discovered their secret: that the *Tirpitz* was no longer at the bottom of Altenfjord.

The usual cry of "Rum-o", which indicated that every man over the age of 18 was entitled to half a tumbler of thick brown issue rum, brought little relief. They were all too much on edge. The lookouts had begun to see non-existent shapes and forms in the blizzard. There were ever more false alarms which made the deck crew even more tense. O'Rourke grew ever angrier at the false reports and threatened the lookout who next made one with "serious trouble".

Now there was no sound save the steady *throb-throb* of the 1,400 h.p. engines and that of the regular pacing of the lookouts on the deck. The men had lost all desire to chat and make the usual cheerful banter of the typical carefree matelot. All of them knew their lives were at stake. Some of the older hands knew that if they were hit and had to spend more than 30 seconds in the freezing green water it meant certain death. They kept the knowledge to themselves, but those who had never sailed these Arctic waters before knew instinctively what would happen to them if they had to go over the side.

It was about four, with the blizzard still raging furiously, when one of the lookouts cried, "*To port, sir . . . a ship!*"

O'Rourke flung up his glasses and even as he did so

he knew they would be of little help in the white-out. This time it was no false alarm. There, wallowing in a trough, was that familiar shape hated by the seamen of a dozen Allied countries, a U-boat! No mistaking it. And it was clear that the U-boat, half-submerged and almost stationary, had not yet spotted them.

O'Rourke acted immediately. "Port 20 . . . full speed ahead!" he yelled down the tube.

The engine-room responded immediately and the motor-launch surged forward through the snow storm, as the crew of the 6-pounder, their lethargy vanished, tensed over their weapon, waiting for the order to fire.

Still viewing the lean shape through his binoculars, O'Rourke could now see men pouring from its conning tower and doubling perilously to the U-boat's own deck-gun. At the conning tower itself a gunner was beginning to swing the twin Oerlikon quick-firer round. They had been spotted!

O'Rourke wasted no more time. He hung out of the bridge door and yelled at the gun crew on the deck below. "Open fire! . . . fire!"

The German Oerlikon gunner beat them to it. Red lights flashed from the submarine's gun-mounting. White zig-zagging lines streaked towards the racing motor-launch, growing in speed by the instant. The length of the British craft's hull was ripped by 20mm rounds. It sounded like a metal rod being run the length of iron railings. Holes appeared everywhere. A seaman on deck screamed and went down in a quivering heap, clutching his face with hands pressed tightly together, through which scarlet blood seeped.

But the gun crew were not deterred by the German fire. They knew they had to hit the U-boat before the enemy gunners could bring the more powerful deck-gun into action. The 6 pounder roared into action and on the monkey island the Vickers gunner peppered the German deck crew with bullets.

The first shell missed. For a moment the U-boat disappeared behind a gout of whirling white water. But the next shell struck home. The U-boat reeled crazily. "Christ, we've hit the sod!" Harding bellowed above the racket, all apprehension vanished now in the wild excitement of the engagement.

The gun crew fired again. At such close range they could hardly miss. The U-boat's turret took a direct hit. The periscope and radio aerials came down. Dead or dying men hung over the side of shattered turret. Yet there was still fight in the U-boat crew.

A star shell exploded above the motor-launch. O'Rourke, just like his gunners, was momentarily blinded. He realised immediately what the U-boat skipper was up to. He was a tricky bastard, trying to pin them down while his torpedomen went into action. He could imagine them working frantically inside the submarine to fire the deadly 'tin fish' from their tubes.

"Gunners – get the bastard – *NOW!*" he yelled frantically, his face whipped by the snow storm.

The gun crew needed no urging. They knew as well as O'Rourke that if they didn't finish off the U-boat in the next few minutes they would be dead men. The torpedoes wouldn't miss their mark at this range. The loader slammed another shell into the smoking breech of the 6 pounder. The gun-layer, fighting that blinding white light from the star shell, peered down his sight. More by instinct than anything else he lined up the submarine once more and pulled the firing bar. The cannon roared. Cherry red flame belched from its muzzle. The motor-launch trembled under the concussion. O'Rourke waited tensely, praying fervently that this time they would sink her. Otherwise – he dare not think the rest of that thought.

The submarine seemed to leap out of the water. Seamen fell over the sides into the freezing sea which would kill them in seconds. With a great splash the U-boat slammed down into the waves once more. Her bow dipped and the two torpedoes she had just fired went hurtling to the bottom.

"This time we've done for the bugger!" Harding cried fervently as the holed U-boat started to go under. "Look at the sod, sir!"

O'Rourke watched mesmerised as the submarine started to slip below the waves at an ever-increasing speed, men jumping from her shattered hull to their certain death. Then she was gone altogether, the only sign that she had ever been there in the first place being the floating debris, the dead men bobbling up and down in the waves she had caused and the great bubbles of air which had been trapped inside her erupting on the surface like huge obscene farts.

Harding's elation vanished. "Poor buggers," he said as they started to steer through the dead bodies of the German submariners. "No use bothering to pick them up. They're dead already."

Suddenly O'Rourke felt Harding's sense of depression. Everyone hated U-boats but the crew were men, men like themselves. Now they were dead, killed not by their fellow men, but by that cruel sea which spared no one whatever his nationality or whether he was good or bad. He bent to the voice tube and ordered the engine-room to reduce speed. The men on both sides were dead already, but he didn't want to feel that the motor-launch's screws were mutilating their corpses.

Their speed dropped and they steered the best they could through the dead Germans and the oil-stained debris from the sunken submarine, all of them suddenly sombre, their sense of elation at their 'kill' vanished as abruptly as it had come.

Still the snowstorm raged, but here and there there were patches of clearer weather, just momentarily, but which for an instant allowed them to see farther ahead. Thus it was that they saw the reason for the submarine's presence in this remote stretch of water.

Slowly, silently a great, lean grey shape passed through a gap in the storm. It was like a ghost ship. O'Rourke felt a cold finger of fear trace its way slowly down his spine as he watched it come and go, moving across their bows. Not a light showed. There was no movement on her huge steel decks. Perhaps there were other U-boats about like the one they had sunk, providing her with her flank guards and escorts. Then she slid back into the snowstorm and was gone.

O'Rourke swallowed hard, almost unable to believe the evidence of his own eyes. "Did you see it too, Chiefie?" he asked in a low awed voice.

"I did," Harding replied, his voice similarly awed.

"And recognise it?"

Harding nodded, as if he could not quite trust himself to speak his answer.

"My God," O'Rourke found his real voice at last. "We've just spotted the biggest warship in the West."

"Ay," Harding said. "The *Tirpitz!*"

Chapter Six

Grand Admiral Doenitz raged. "*Idioten!*" he roared into the red scrambler phone. "*Total Idioten!*" With difficulty he controlled himself and listened to what the admiral in charge of Oslo was saying. When the latter was finished he barked, his icy blue eyes blazing with anger, "I want an inquiry made. Whoever is responsible for this will have to be punished, severely punished. Heads must roll, do you understand?" With that he slammed the receiver back down in its cradle and breathing hard turned to face his assembled staff in his big Murwik office, while outside the new recruits to the *Kriegsmarine* practised the goose-step on the barracks square. They waited apprehensively. Doenitz's fiery temper was notorious throughout the German Navy.

"*Meine Herren,*" he announced, containing himself with the greatest difficulty, "there has been a colossal blunder in Norway. The British have penetrated Altenfjord and thus know that the *Tirpitz* has been refloated. It is assumed that the same British have just sunk one of the U-boats escorting the *Tirpitz*. They might well have seen the ship itself. Our great plan, therefore, is in extreme danger. What is to be done?"

Doenitz stared hard around their grim, set faces. All of them knew that one British ship now endangered

Germany's chance of ending the war in the Fatherland's favour. One single enemy ship.

Von Puttkammer, the most senior commander among the group, cleared his throat and said, "We must assume that this English ship will break radio silence and relay its information to London even before it reaches England."

Doenitz nodded his agreement. "That has already been taken into account, von Puttkammer. It is a good point. Our whole listening service is on alert for any message sent from that part of the North Sea. So far nothing has been picked up."

"Yes, Grand Admiral," von Puttkammer said. "But once they do send, we can pin-point their position and destroy them, if not by sea, then by air."

"I shall alert the Sixth Air Fleet in Holland immediately." Doenitz nodded to his immaculately uniformed aide with his gold lanyard, the badge of his office. "See to it, Heinz," he commanded.

Hastily the elegant young officer left the room to carry out the order, as Doenitz said, "I have also alerted all remaining U-boats in the North Sea area. But as you know, gentlemen, the British appeared to have broken the strength of our U-Boat arm. I fear they have little chance of intercepting this British vessel without being attacked themselves. But I know my brave boys," he added proudly, "they'll attack all the same, even if it means their own deaths."

The officers fell silent for a while as they pondered the problem. Outside, the drill instructor was bellowing, "Come on, you pisspot men! Open those legs. Nothing will fall out. If they do, I'll pick 'em for yer." No one in the room smiled.

"Grand Admiral," a voice broke the heavy, tense

silence. It was Carlsohn, one of the great aces of the U-boat service, his tunic heavy with decorations, the Knight's Cross of the Iron Cross dangling from his throat. Despite the U-boat skipper's protests, Doenitz had ordered him on to the staff. He didn't want to risk the young ace's life any more. The Fatherland would need men like Carlsohn after the war. "*Ja, Kapitanleutnant?*" Doenitz said, a wintry smile on his thin bitter face, for he was very fond of the handsome young U-boat skipper.

"Well, sir," Carlsohn said, aware that all the senior officers, many of whom were twice his age, were watching him. "I think we can assume that this Tommy boat will be heading for the nearest British port with his info. It's red hot and he'll be wanting to get it off his chest as soon as possible."

"Yes, I think you're right," Doenitz said, nodding.

"Well, sir," Carlsohn continued, "if that's the case, he'll be heading for Scotland. They're the closest. Last December we launched a V1 attack on Northern England with the missiles being launched from Heinkel III bombers from *Kampfgruppe 53*. It wasn't very successful because it was the first time it had ever been done. The pilots not only had to fly the attack, but they also had to ignite the engine of the one-ton missile before launching it. It was a very tricky procedure."

"Yes, I remember the attack," Doenitz said thoughtfully. "We did manage, if I remember correctly, to inflict serious damage on some English town near Manchester."

"Oldham, sir," Carlsohn said promptly.

"Yes. Well, go on Carlsohn."

"Well, sir, if we launch a similar attack on the northern Scottish ports the Tommies might head for, we could at least destroy communications for a time and with a bit of luck get the Tommies in question as well."

The young U-boat ace waited expectantly as Doenitz considered the suggestion. Finally the Grand Admiral made his decision. "This project is of such vital importance to Germany that we must use all measures at our disposal to prevent the Tommies learning about the *Tirpitz*. This is what I have decided. All air, sea forces will join in the hunt for the British. At the same time we will launch an aerial V1 attack as suggested by the *Kapitanleutnant*." He flashed a glance at his wrist-watch, which the Führer himself had given him. "It is now exactly 0800 hours. By 1200 I want all plans formulated and operational orders issued to the units concerned." He looked at the staff with those stern blue eyes of his. "Gentlemen, we cannot afford to fail. The future of the Fatherland depends upon our success. Is that quiet clear?"

There was a murmur of assent.

Doenitz snapped, "Well, gentlemen, to your posts. There is work to be done."

The officers clicked to attention and picking up their caps and briefcases filed out hastily. Doenitz sat down, suddenly exhausted. Why, he didn't know. Perhaps it was the emotional strain of knowing that if he failed Germany would be lost. Then he pulled himself together. He picked up the phone and barked, "Get me the Führer's Headquarters. This is a most urgent, priority-one call." He slammed the phone down and waited.

One minute later it rang again and when he lifted the receiver a voice said, "The Führer will speak to Grand Admiral Doenitz." Then that familiar Austrian voice growled, "Well Doenitz, what is so important?"

"*Mein Führer,*" Doenitz answered, rising from his

chair and clicking to attention as if he were physically in Hitler's presence. "I have an explanation to make." Hastily he told Hitler what he had heard from Oslo half an hour before and the counter-measures he had just taken, then he waited for Hitler's reaction

"You have done very well, my dear Doenitz," Hitler said after a moment. "But we must try to stop the enemy learning any more of our project. When will the *Tirpitz* be ready for operations?"

"Very soon, *mein Führer*. We have a full crew under an excellent captain. In the trials we are holding at this moment she has proved herself to be in excellent shape. The bombing badly damaged her engines. They have been repaired, but don't have the power they once did. Still, she is fast enough for the proposed mission – and one thing is very certain, *mein Führer*," he added significantly, "there is not an English warship within 3,000 kilometres of here which is capable of tackling the *Tirpitz*."

"Excellent, excellent!" Hitler growled. "Soon that drunken sot will be leaving Russia and flying back to his own country. By then you must be prepared. We shall have only this one opportunity of liquidating the swine."

"Have no fear, *mein Führer*," Doenitz said, "we shall be ready on the day."

"I am sure you will, Doenitz. Now all I can wish you is *Hals und Beinbruch*."*

"Thank you, *mein Führer*."

The line went dead and Doenitz relaxed once more. He sat down, his mind racing.

Half an hour later Doenitz's phone rang again. This

* Literally "Break your neck and bones", ie 'happy landings' in English.

time it was von Puttkammer on the other end. His voice sounded elated as he said, "*Herr Grossadmiral*, we've had a quite extraordinary bit of luck!"

"What?" Doenitz said eagerly.

"A Condor weather plane returning from a mission has suffered some damage to its engines, forcing it to come down low over the sea."

"Yes, go on," Doenitz snapped impatiently.

"Well, sir, the pilot thinks he's spotted the Tommy. He had received the general signal to be on the lookout for a British craft which he had heard had been damaged by us in Altenfjord. Well this craft had a damaged superstructure and a makeshift radio mast. It was limping along towards the coast of Scotland. He lost the vessel after a few minutes when the snow came back, but the pilot was nearly 100 per cent certain that it was the craft we are looking for."

Like an excited child, Doenitz clapped his skinny hands together at the news. "Marvellous . . . marvellous!" he exclaimed in delight. "Put every surface craft into operation to follow up from that last position."

"The V1s?" von Puttkammer queried.

Doenitz considered for a moment then said, "Yes, get the attack launched on the Scottish ports. It will help to confuse the English and certainly prevent them from giving any aid to this lone Tommy when we find him."

"It will be done, *Herr Grossadmiral*." The phone went dead.

Doenitz sat back in his chair and stared at his own lean face in the mirror opposite. The Tommy was trapped. He wouldn't get away a second time. He beamed at himself happily.

PART THREE

The Russian Takes a Hand

Chapter One

"She was a dancer from the Romany Theatre," Beria said, peering up at the aide through his rimless pince-nez. "Big, juicy with wonderfully athletic thighs. I thought she was going to squeeze the very life out of me with them about my body during the act. But it was an experience, Comrade Colonel. I hope only that you can duplicate the experience for me tonight with that gypsy girl you have promised. They are usually very primitive and highly sexed."

His aide, Colonel Sarkisov, said in his usual oily fashion, "I think you can rely on me, Comrade Beria. I don't think you'll have to use drugs or the knout on her to make her willing either."

The two men laughed and standing to one side Lieutenant Commander Sarov's face hardened even more. Even in the midst of total war Beria, the head of the Russian Secret Police, could not go without his nightly orgy here in Moscow. He still had to have his 'green fruit', as he called the virginal girls that his aides snatched from the streets of Moscow so that he could drug or beat them with his knout till they were dripping with blood and he was excited enough to be able to perform. The man was a monster. One day Comrade Stalin would undoubtedly do away with him when he had served his purpose.

Beria still continued to ignore him. Deliberately, Sarov couldn't help thinking. It was his usual manner of humiliating those who were his subordinates. He stared down at the obscene photos his aide had just put on the enormous desk. "That one has an arse like a black silk cushion," he said pointing one of them, depicting two women toying with each other. "I bet you could sink into it up to your loins."

The aide sniggered and said in his wheedling voice, "A waste on another woman, Comrade, eh?"

"Perhaps. But as a stimulant to the watcher," Beria said in that soft female voice of his, "a useful act." He sniffed and then swept the photos aside. A couple fell to the floor, but Beria appeared not to notice. Obediently, his aide and procurer picked them up.

Beria appeared to see Sarov as if it were for the first time. "You were wounded in the Black Sea, Comrade Commander, and have, I hear, been declared unfit for any further active service. Is that true?"

"Yes Comrade."

Beria took in the rows of medal ribbons on Sarov's chest, and remarked, "I see you are not a coward. You have many medals for bravery."

Sarov said nothing, but his bewilderment at why he had been summoned to the Moscow HQ of the Secret Police increased.

"I believe, too," Beria continued, staring at the young officer with those evil dark eyes of his, "that you speak excellent English?"

"I was an honours graduate in English from the University of Moscow before the war, Comrade," Sarov replied, his bewilderment increasing.

"*Horoscho*," Beria said in Russian, then he turned to the aide and spoke to him in his native Georgian which

Sarov naturally didn't understand though he suspected they were talking about him. Finally the aide nodded as if he was agreeing to something and Beria turned to face Sarov once more. "What I am about to tell you now is a state secret. To reveal it to a second party is a crime which would be punished by death. You clearly understand that, Comrade Commander," he said severely, this time speaking in English.

"Yes, Comrade, I understand," the young naval officer said, though he didn't understand at all. He tensed and waited for what was to come.

"At this present moment," Beria started to explain, "there is a great secret conference of the Allied leaders taking place at Yalta in the Crimea. Comrade Secretary Stalin is discussing with the heads of two capitalist states, America and Britain, the future of Europe. It is obvious that Roosevelt is dying. He, therefore, is not much of a hindrance to Comrade Stalin. Europe is of not much interest to the Americans as it is. They want to pull their soldiers out of the Continent as soon as they can and get on with their war in Japan. Churchill is different. As perhaps you know, Churchill has been an implacable enemy of Mother Russia ever since our glorious revolution. Now he is insisting the French must take part in any future discussions, only because he wants the French Army to support him. In addition, he is attempting to stop Comrade Stalin's plans for Poland. And so it goes on. He argues virtually every point with Comrade Stalin. So," Beria paused and looked hard at the puzzled naval officer, *Churchill must die!*"

Sarov looked shocked. He had known of Churchill's role during the Allied intervention in Russia after the Revolution. But that was long ago. Since 1941 he had come to see Churchill as a valuable ally of Russia's.

Now he had to die – and what had this man's death to do with him?

Beria saw the shocked look on Sarov's face and chuckled. It wasn't a pleasant sound. "Don't worry! It wouldn't be wise to kill him in Russia. It would be even stupider for us to do the killing. No, the Fritzes are the ones who will carry out the murder. Our hands will be completely clean." Suddenly there was iron in the monster's voice. "But die he must!"

"But what is this to do with me, Comrade?" Sarov stuttered.

"This. We are afraid that the British Secret Service is starting to get to know too much about the German plan, of which we are informed through our agents in Germany. It is imperative that they do not find out the full details before the Germans put their plan into operation. Churchill would be saved and remain a thorn in Comrade Stalin's side. Our plans for Europe and the future of communism would be stymied time and time again. So we are sending you to London as our assistant naval attaché." He gave Sarov a cold smile. "Now what do you say to that, Comrade?"

"It is a great honour . . . at my age," Sarov managed to say, completely out of his depth.

"We have great faith in you. You are brave and resourceful. You speak their language and you are a naval officer, who knows all about naval matters. I have read your full secret police dossier." He tapped the file in front of him. "I know everything about you. Time is pressing. So I will tell what your task will be in England. As a diplomat you will have full diplomatic immunity so you can travel everywhere, see and do everything."

Outside there was a deep bass boom and the sudden

blare of brass. It was the Guards band leading another battalion to the station, from whence it would journey to the front. Since Stalingrad Stalin had ordered that the civilians should see just how strong the Red Army was. He had said that it would inspire the civilians to ever greater efforts. But as Sarov waited he could hear only a few feeble cheers from the Muscovites. They didn't have the strength; they were too weak and weary. The war had been going on too long.

Beria frowned suddenly, as if he were annoyed by the lack of interest outside. He had his secret police everywhere. They would undoubtedly report to him later who the lazy malcontents were who had refused to cheer their own brave boys in uniform.

"Now," he continued as the thud of the drum and blare of brass died away, followed by that of the marching feet, rank after rank of cannon-fodder for the front in Germany, "we have pinpointed the man who is trying to ascertain what the Fritzes are up to." He took a file from his desk and handed it to Sarov. "In there are all available details of the man in question, who by the way is a naval officer like yourself." He gave Sarov a crooked smile as the latter accepted the dossier. "The Englishman seems, as you will see in due course, to have a few peculiar sexual, tastes. No matter. That officer is the one that you will ensure is eliminated."

"*Eliminated* . . . I?"

"Do not worry, Comrade Sarov. You will not have to do that. You are a Russian. We can't go round killing our allies, can we? Especially if we were to be found out." Again he gave the other man that crooked grin of his. "No, it will be your job to ensure that the liquidation is carried out, that's all. And by an English citizen. It will have to look like an ordinary

103

murder, not a political assassination. We must remain in the background, simply pulling strings unseen, like a puppet-master above the stage. You understand?"

Sarov was too shocked to reply. Suddenly it dawned upon him that he was being ordered to assist in a murder! Why him? He was an honest, decent naval officer who had fought with clean hands for the past three years in the Baltic and Black Sea. In his craft there had been no murder of German survivors as there had been in other ships of the Black Sea Fleet. Now he was being asked to dirty his hands by murdering some unknown Englishman!

With an effort of sheer naked willpower he pulled himself together. What would happen if he refused this task? He didn't need a crystal ball to answer that. He now knew a great state secret. If he refused, Beria wouldn't even allow him to leave this very office with that knowledge. He would be arrested at once. Within the day he might well be dead. That was the manner of the NKVD, the Secret Police. They buried their secrets. War hero that he was, personally decorated by Stalin, wouldn't stop them. What did such pieces of coloured enamel mean to them? It wouldn't even be a gulag, one of those terrible and remote work camps in Siberia. He might escape with his tremendous secret from such a place. Oh no, it would be the sudden bullet at the base of his skull as he crouched on his knees in some underground cell. That would be that. They'd bury him in lime in the prison courtyard and he would have disappeared for ever.

Sarov's brain raced as he tried to come to the right decision. Once he was in London he might be able to defect, become a 'submarine', as the saying went in Moscow, go underground. That way he wouldn't have to carry out the terrible mission these monsters with their perverted tastes and unlimited powers had assigned to him.

"Well?" Beria demanded impatiently.

Sarov swallowed hard. He had made his decision. "I shall be honoured to accept this task for the Motherland, Comrade," he heard himself saying from far, far away.

"Good! Then it's done." Beria turned and snapped something in Georgian to the aide.

The latter nodded and said in Russian, "A flight to London has been arranged for you from Moscow Airport this noon. In an hour you will be given all you need, diplomatic passport, accreditation, English money, gold sovereigns for bribes, and so on. While these things are being prepared for you, Comrade Commander, you will go outside into the anteroom and prepare yourself a little by reading the dossier on this Englishman from their Naval Intelligence."

"Thank you, Comrade," he heard himself saying, hardly recognising the voice as his own.

Beria waved his hand. He was dismissed.

Hastily he saluted and with the dossier under his arm strode out of the huge office, his head reeling. Behind him Beria was saying, "There is something about young virgins, dear Comrade. They give a man of – er – certain age a feeling of power. You know the way you pull their skinny knees apart and they feel it for the very first time. Like a wild horse being put to the saddle to break it in—"

Sarov went into the little outer office where he had waited before, the walls hung with pictures of hard-faced men, who according to the legend had given their lives for the 'cause of the glorious revolution'. With fingers that trembled badly, he opened the file to be confronted by a photograph of a broken-nosed man with a long, haughty face, dressed in naval uniform. It had been taken by a telephoto-lense in some busy street, perhaps in London. The man looked hard and as if he knew his business. He was with a pretty older woman dressed in what appeared to be tiger skin coat: a woman of the kind which he suspected no longer existed in Russia, even for the Party bosses.

A *poule de luxe*, he remembered the French called such women. The Englishman had expensive tastes. Then his eyes fell on the name beneath the street photograph. It was 'Lt. Commander Ian Fleming, R.N.V.R'.

He stared hard at it, as if trying to etch the name on his brain. So that was the Englishman he was going to help kill.

Chapter Two

"Sodding corned beef and stale bread a bloody agen!" Sparks grumbled, as the dirty-aproned cook placed the big tin platter on the heaving mess table. "Yer know what yer can do with frigging fodder like that!"

CPO Harding, who was passing through the mess, looked hard at him. "You should thank God yer've got that, Sparks. Tomorrow, if we're still at sea, it'll be hard tack. We've run out of grub."

Sparks took a sip of the scalding-hot cocoa from his chipped brown mug and asked, "D'yer think we will, Chiefie? I thought we'd make it by nightfall."

"Not now. The weather's against us. They're losing power down in the engine-room as well."

"Right ray of frigging sunshine," Sparks commented under his breath and then with a weary sigh dug his fork into the greasy slab of corned beef.

Harding looked round the circle of faces in the dim light of the crowded mess. They were very tired, he could see that, their eyes bloodshot with the strain, their faces haggard, most of them dirty and unshaven. He knew why. In the ablutions the flannel was like a board with the freezing cold and the soap had frozen to the zinc tops. Most of the men contented themselves with a cat's lick, not even taking their uniforms off to sleep in their hammocks. In fact, he could smell them. But, he told himself, they were a good lot.

"Harry," he said to the hairy sailor about to dish out the Spotty Dick pudding, "see if yer can't get a bit o' music on that radio of yourn. Cheer this bloody miserable lot up a bit."

"Yes, Chiefie," the hairy sailor agreed readily enough. He bent over the battered radio which he had bought for ten bob from a dockie, who said he'd 'found' it after a raid on Hull's James Street, and fiddled with the dials. There was a blur of brass band music, followed by some-one ranting in German, which in its turn was followed by that well-known smarmy, supposedly upper-class voice, "Jarmainy calling . . . Jarmairy calling . . ."

"It's frigging Lord Haw Haw," Sparks exclaimed. "Wonder what that sod's got to say for himself today?"

"They say he knows everything," somebody chimed in. "By gum, I remember the time he said our local town hall clock had stopped and Christ it had! How did he know that, eh?"

"You think that for you in England, ladies and gentlemen, the war is virtually over," Lord Haw Haw was saying. "The Home Guard is being stood down. The blackout has been changed to a dim-out. We Germans will never attack again. That is what you think. But you are mistaken. Soon you, in particular, on the north-east coast will find out just how powerful we Germans still are. You will learn to your cost—"

"Oh put a frigging sock in it!" Sparks moaned. "Turn 'im off! Find some music or sommat."

Harding looked at their weary faces as the hairy sailor fiddled with the dial. Lord Haw Haw's statement had hit home. All of them were from the north-East coast. For years their families had suffered from the daily German attacks on it. Now they were worried; even though the pundits were saying the war was over, the Germans perhaps had something up their sleeves and it was all going to start once more. It was with a near sense of relief that Harding heard the alarm gongs begin to clatter their warning and the mess deck was suddenly turned into controlled chaos as the men began frantically to pull on their battle gear.

The Junkers came in at sea level, about 50 of them, seeming to skim over the waves, long cylinder-like objects fastened beneath their fuselages. "Holy cow," O'Rourke gasped when he saw the first line come winging across the sea. "It's the whole German air force!"

Harding, next to him, helmet placed squarely on his grizzled head, put down his binoculars. "Can't make 'em out, sir. What's those cylinders beneath them?"

"Search me, Chiefie. Somehow though I don't think they're looking for us. But those two bloody Focke-Wulfs 190s behind the first wave are. Look they're peeling off!"

The two stubby, radial-engined fighter-bombers were now leaving the main formation, throttled back and lowering their undercarriages in order to reduce their speed even more. It was a clear indication that they were about attack the motor-launch.

The gunners knew that, too. Everywhere they swung their weapons round to port, as the Germans prepared to assault from the flank, so that they would have the largest possible target.

Now as the great force of Junkers thundered past, their prop wash churning the water into a white, angry maelstrom, heading for the coast, the Focke-Wulfs came in, cannon spitting angry white flame. Tracer shells started to hiss lethally towards the battered craft.

Instantly, O'Rourke realised he needed help. He would have to break radio silence at last. "Chiefie!" he yelled frantically. "Tell Sparks to send out a mayday with our position. Ask for immediate help."

"Sir." Harding moved out of the wheelhouse with surprising speed for such an old man, clattering down the steps as if he were an 18-year-old.

Cannon shells ripped the length of the superstructure. There was the smell of burning. A rating pitched down clutching his shattered knee and moaning piteously. Then the first attacker was zooming over them, dragging its black shadow with it across the deck, to zoom up into the sky in preparation for another attack.

An instant later the second Focke-Wulf came roaring in, churning up the water as it zipped across the surface of the sea. A wall of fire rose to meet it. The pilot pressed home his attack undeterred. Suddenly, an anxious, tense O'Rourke on the bridge, watching the attack cried, "Oh, no! Not that bloody well too!" The Focke-Wulf was carrying several small bombs under its wings. Next moment the pilot released them and they came tumbling down.

A series of great spouts of water came hurrying ever closer to the motor-launch. There was a tremendous boom and the searing, ripping sound of metal being shattered. The motor-launch rocked violently. Its engines stopped and abruptly the launch was wallowing in the water and O'Rourke's nostrils were filled with the acrid and nauseous stink of a burning ship. Up on deck, the Russian fugitives who had probably never been on a ship in their lives panicked. They started to wail and wring their hands, tears of self-pity streaming down their worn cheeks. O'Rourke didn't understand their language but he knew what they were saying, "We're sinking . . . we're sinking!" And O'Rourke knew they were right.

They were.

Slowly the launch started to list to port. Already O'Rourke could hear water gurgling inside the hull. Now, he knew, they were a sitting duck. The two enemy fighter-bombers could finish them off at their leisure. And the German pilots also knew it. Almost lazily they curved in the grey sky and readied themselves for the final approach. O'Rourke knew this was the end. He cupped his hands around his mouth and yelled from the shattered bridge, "*Prepare to abandon ship! Prepare—*"

Abruptly the cry died on his lips. He stared at the sky to port, as if he couldn't believe the evidence of his own eyes. The second Focke-Wulfe was suddenly on fire, screaming towards the sea, trailing thick brown smoke, flecked with cherry red flames. What had happened?

Then he saw their saviours: two white-painted Sunderlands of Coastal Command, turret machine-guns blazing, were coming in behind the unsuspecting Germans, intent only on their victims. "Stand by lads!" he cried, his voice abruptly full of hope. "It's Coastal Command!"

Flaps down to reduce speed, the FW190s were near stalling speed and were totally unprepared for this attack from the rear.

A ragged cheer rose from the stunned men, which gained in intensity as the second four-engined flying boat tackled the German plane from the rear.

Again the German pilot was too intent on finishing off the 'sitting duck' to flash a glance in his rear-view mirror and spot the two great flying boats lumbering down upon him. Now it was the German's turn to be the sitting duck. The Sunderlands opened fire where it was impossible to miss. Down below, the crew of the sinking ship could see the chunks of metal flying from the Focke-Wulf as the bullets struck home. Black smoke started to pour from the enemy plane. Suddenly its engine coughed and stopped, shattered by that savage burst of fire.

Desperately the pilot fought to keep his plane airborne. O'Rourke could imagine it, his face contorted with horror as he attempted to re-start the engine. To no avail! His speed decreased rapidly as he lost height in a shallow glide. The Coastal Command planes were relentless. They pressed home their advantage, their Browning machine-guns hammering away. Then the pilot of the German plane lost control altogether. Perhaps he was already dead. Like a stone the plane fell out of the sky and splashed into the water. No one got out.

Minutes later, with only the deck of the shattered motor-launch above water, the Sunderlands touched down, feathering their four props to avoid creating any turbulence which would sink the stricken craft. On the deck the relieved matelots cheered and waved. Next to them the slave workers from Russia were hugging each other and crying at the same time.

A face appeared in the cockpit and the co-pilot shouted through a loud-hailer, "Nearly got yer feet wet then, chaps! What?"

"Dr Livingstone, I presume?" O'Rourke said weakly.

"Something like that," the voice replied. "Hang on half a mo. We'll soon have you aboard then we'll be having tiffin. Hope you're properly dressed!"

O'Rourke turned to Harding and said with a sigh of relief, "I don't think he's the world's greatest comic, but I could kiss him at this very moment."

Harding grinned and answered, *Kiss him, sir*? I've fallen in love with him. I'm gonna get shut of the old woman and frigging well marry him!"

Ten minutes later they were all crowded into the fuselages of the two flying boats, sipping hot tea from the crews' thermos flasks, then winging their way westwards. They were going home.

Chapter Three

"All hell has been let loose," a harassed, unshaven Fleming exclaimed to Lt. Commander Keith as he sat there in his crowded little office at the side of the docks.

Howling Mad looked at the Intelligence man with a certain amount of disdain. Officers should never be unshaven even in the most trying of circumstances. There had been times of great stress when he had shaved in cold tea – once even in a glass of beer – so that his crew could see that everything was normal; the skipper was shaving as usual. "How do you mean?" he asked. "All hell has been let loose?"

"Half an hour ago the Hun started bombarding the Scottish east coast ports with V1s. A great fleet of Hun planes came across the North Sea at wave-top height so that we couldn't pick them up on the radar. We only caught them on the screens when they started to climb to obtain sufficient height to launch the flying bombs. Ten of them were shot down," Fleming added with a shrug, as if it didn't matter very much.

"Hm," Howling Mad said and waited for what else the smooth grandee had to tell him.

Fleming plunged on. "Then the air is full of coded messages to their surface and underwater craft. We're picking up their cyphers all the time. It seems as if the

Hun naval high command has alerted every damned ship they've got in North Sea for a special mission."

"Do we know what it is, this special mission?" Howling Mad asked, leaning forward and suddenly very interested. Outside, the whistles and hooters were shrilling to indicate the dock workers knocking off for their midday break. Slowly groups of them were heading for the sheds to have their sandwiches and tea from bottles. Others, flush with money still, were heading for the pubs in Hedon Road to down a pint before the beer ran out, which it usually did at lunchtime.

"Yes," Fleming answered, "our decoders tell us—"

He was interrupted by the shrilling of the phone on Keith's desk. Impatiently the latter picked it up and barked, "Lieutenant Commander Keith here." Then Keith's face, angry at being disturbed in the middle of his conversation with Fleming, was transformed. "Say that again," he demanded. Then, when his informant repeated the news, Keith actually smiled and chortled, "Bloody good show! Yes, yes, we'll be there." He put the phone down and announced happily, "They've picked up O'Rourke and his crew – and apparently half a dozen Russkis too, though God knows where he found them!"

For once Fleming's Etonian gravitas deserted him. "What did you say, Keith?" he stuttered. "I don't quite understand. Please say again."

"That was Coastal Command at Lossiemouth," Howling Mad barked, as if he were talking to some village idiot. "Two of their kites picked up O'Rourke and his chaps after knocking out two Focke-Wulfs which had just sunk his ship. They're on their way here now. Two Sunderland flying boats, unlikely though that is. They're going to land in the Humber. Apparently O'Rourke has got some vital news for us." He rose to his feet, pulled on his greatcoat and slung his gas mask over his shoulder. "Come on Fleming, let's not sit there like a spare one at a wedding. They'll be here in a brace of shakes."

Fleming tamely followed.

The midday shoppers crowded the quay in the centre of Hull as the two great white-painted flying boats taxied their way up the estuary. Over these last few years the harassed citizens of Hull had seen many strange things, but it was the first time that Sunderland flying boats had been spotted coming up the Humber right to the centre of the badly hit city.

Standing in the front row next to Howling Mad, Fleming could hear the excited gossip all around him, the queries, the comments. A turbanned matron, with steel curlers peeping out from beneath the cloth, was saying, "I bet it's something to do with the parade. Perhaps there's gonna be a fly over."

"Get off, yer daft ha'porth!" her companion, a skinny woman who clutched her ration book in her hand tightly as if someone might steal it at any moment, replied, "Yer don't fly-over with them big things. Yer have Spitfires and Hurricanes and such like."

For a moment Fleming was puzzled by the conversation. "What parade?" he asked himself. Hadn't those Home Guards watching over the Hun prisoner talked about a parade too? Then he dismissed the matter as the hatch of the first flying boat opened to reveal a battered-looking O'Rourke standing there.

"The Navy's here!" someone in the crowd yelled loudly at the sight and the throng roared at the memory of that famous day back at the beginning of the war when a

116

Royal Navy captain had uttered those same words when his ship had stopped the German prison-ship *Altmark* and rescued the captured British merchantmen on their way to POW camps.

O'Rourke grinned wearily and then as the launch drew parallel to the flying boat's entrance hatch, he stepped gingerly into it, telling himself that if he fell into the drink now he'd never live it down. The others followed as a second launch drew up by the other flying Sunderland.

For some reason the crowd began to cheer and cry "Hip . . . hip . . . *hurrah!*" Some clapped. "What a great lot of lads they are!" the matron in the turban gushed.

Howling Mad looked for a moment as if he were going to start baying in one of his crazy moods. Then he realised they were cheering his men and suddenly he looked quite pleased, or as pleased as he could ever be. He nodded his approval.

Then O'Rourke was clambering up the wet, dripping iron ladder to the quay. At the top he snapped to attention and touched his hand to his battered, seawater-stained cap in salute, while the matron whispered to her companion with the ration book, "Ain't he handsome, that young officer!"

Howling Mad waited till they were all on the quay, including the Russians. But he frowned in bewilderment when he saw them in what looked like striped pyjamas, before snapping to Harding, "Chiefie, march the party off to the station buffet up there," he indicated Paragon Street. "Here," he pulled a white five-pound note from his wallet and then added another one. "Give 'em beer and whatever wads there are left. I'll arrange transport as soon as I can get to the phone in the Station Hotel."

"Thank you, sir," Harding snapped and, though his

poor old knees were hurting like hell, he swung round smartly, as if he were still a young leading seaman full of 'piss and vinegar', and cried: "Party will come to attention *attenshun!*"

They stamped to attention, including the Russians, though they did so a few seconds later than the rest.

"By the right now!" Harding commanded, his breath fogging on the cold air. "Quick march! Eyes right!"

Gravely the three officers snapped to attention, raising their hands to their caps as the ragged, oil-stained survivors swung by them heading for the buffet.

"Swing them arms . . . bags of swank now . . . remember who you are!" Harding chivied them, as if they were back in training at Portsmouth, and the ragged Russians imitated their exaggerated arm-swinging as best they could.

"Makes tears come to your eyes," the matron with the steel curlers whispered and dabbed her eyes with a dirty handkerchief. "Them poor lads, what might they have been through!"

Five minutes later, in the station buffet, Sparks was urging at the ancient barmaid, "Wallop all round, Luv! Heaven help a sailor on a night like this!" Then the three officers got out of the staff car and walked into the entrance of the Station Hotel, watched by the little man in the blue suit. Fleming ordered pink gins – "doubles, please!" – which flustered the old waiter. In years nobody had ordered a double pink gin, even admirals, but then he saw the look in Fleming's eyes and decided it would be wiser to get the drinks.

Fleming and Howling Mad waited till he had brought the gins, then Keith said, looking around to check whether they were being observed, "All right, young O'Rourke, fire away! What did you find out?"

O'Rourke didn't even bother to taste his gin. He was eager to get the startling news off his chest at last. Without any preamble, he blurted out, "The Jerries have raised her. They've brought the *Tirpitz* up. I know, because we saw her. No mistaking her at all. Straight out of the illustration in 'Jane's Fighting Ships'!"

Fleming whistled softly and Howling Mad snorted, "Oh my frigging sainted aunt! That means we've got the West's most powerful battleship loose again in the North Atlantic!"

O'Rourke nodded his agreement and then took a greedy gulp at the potent pink gin. "'Fraid you have, sir," he gasped as the gin took his breath away. Then he started to tell the two senior officers what had happened in the Altenfjord.

When he had finished, Fleming asked, "Do your Ruskies know anything about what the Hun is going to do with the *Tirpitz*?" He puffed out a stream of blue smoke from the ivory cigarette holder.

"Apparently not, sir. There's only one of them who speaks a bit of English, a chap called Levy."

Fleming's nose wrinkled in disdain. "Jew, eh," he commented.

O'Rourke ignored the comment. "I thought perhaps if we could get a fluent Russian speaker up here, toot-sweet, we might be able to interrogate them better than I could and get more out of them."

"Will do," Fleming agreed. "This very day."

For a few moments they lapsed into silence, enjoying their strong gin. In the foyer a string trio was playing something from the *Mikado*. O'Rourke told himself what a different world that was.

Howling Mad said, suddenly worried, "I think their Lordships ought to be informed as soon as possible, don't you, Fleming? We haven't got a capital ship left on this side of the world. If the *Tirpitz* gets loose . . ." He left the rest of his sentence unspoken.

Fleming nodded. "There's the RAF," he suggested.

"In the kind of weather we get off these coasts at this time of the year, Fleming?" Howling Mad snorted scornfully. "Come off it!"

"What do you mean?"

"Listen, Fleming. The only way the Brylcreem boys are going to tackle the *Tirpitz* is get out of the range of her ack-ack and gain, at the same time, sufficient height to drop their 12,000-pounds bombs. If they're too low they go up with the bomb. Now at this time of the year with the fogs and the snowstorms and the rotten kind of weather we generally get, they wouldn't even be able to see the bloody *Tirpitz* from the right bombing height. And let me tell you this, Fleming," Howling Mad thrust out his jaw pugnaciously, "nothing but a bloody direct hit by a 12,000 lb Tallboy will stop the *Tirpitz*".

Watching them in the mirror behind the reception while old Joe shuffled back and forth, looking as if he were working, though the little man knew that the cunning old sod had a bottle of rum in the backroom from which he took sips at regular intervals, the little man in the shiny blue suit told himself that things were coming to a head. He had seen the survivors march into the station buffet. Now here was O'Rourke, all flushed and excited, looking as if he'd been through the mill, while the other two senior men listened to him as if he were frigging Churchill himself. Even that upperclass sod Fleming showed some excitement. Yes, it was time to report to Igor. Things were on the move. "Be seeing yer, Joe," he called. "Keep yer eyes skinned and yer lugs pinned back! I'm slinging me hook. If yer a good old fart I'll bring yer another bottle of rum for the back room."

"Yer know I don't drink," Joe quavered, fearful that the manager might have overheard.

"Like fuck, yer don't. Ta, ta, Joe!" With that he was gone.

Chapter Four

Sarov was puzzled. He stood in front of the exit of Croydon Airport looking for the car which his Embassy was supposed to have sent for him. But there was nothing there. Indeed the whole street was deserted save for what seemed to be some official vehicle scurrying away at the end of the road with its bell jingling. Something was wrong. He had been on naval active service long enough to 'feel' when violence and danger were imminent. He had that same feeling now, but what could be happening in this South London suburb so far away from the fighting fronts?

He put down his little case, filled with bottles of pepper vodka and the long, paper-tipped *pappiroska* cigarettes that the Embassy had requested he should bring for them. He didn't know quite what to do. How was he going to get to the Embassy without an official car? He didn't even know where the place was.

Far to the east above the sea of house roofs he could hear the sound of muffled gunfire. Tiny puffballs of anti-aircraft shells exploding in the dreary winter sky told him that some kind of air-raid was going on. What was the explanation for the absence of the Embassy car and emptiness of the place?

Now he became aware of the strange sound coming from the sky in the south-east. It was a kind of slow chug-chug, like the noise an old-fashioned two-stroke motor-cycle engine might make. He frowned. What could it be, he couldn't identify the sound at all. He raised his head under the big-peaked cap of an officer in the Red Navy and searched the sky systematically like he would on active service in the Black Sea trying to spot a Fritz raider.

Then he saw it. A long, cyclinder-like object skimming over the the rooftops, spurts of red flame coming from what looked like an exhaust. What in three devils' names was it, he asked himself. Was it some kind of aircraft? If it was, he had never seen its like ever before.

Abruptly, with a great rush of sound, a plane which he *did* recognise zoomed across the sky at a tremendous speed heading straight for the strange flying object. A Hurricane, he said to himself. He knew the British-made plane well. They had had some of them stationed on the Black Sea coast to protect the Red Fleet.

Sarov watched in amazement as the British fighter approached the strange object from behind, on what appeared to be a collision course. Then the Hurricane pulled alongside the thing and began a roll, so that its port wing-tip caught the stubby starboard wing of the strange flying object. Sarov held his breath. Would the Hurricane crash? No! The pilot righted his plane and zoomed upwards in a climb as the cyclinder with the red flame coming form its exhaust, abruptly tipped over. Almost immediately the flame went out and the strange put-put noise stopped.

"Get yer bloody head down, man!" an angry voice broke the sudden silence. "The bastard's coming down!"

Heavy shoes clattered across the tarmac. Before he was aware of what was going on, a hefty middle-aged woman came running across to him, clutching her helmeted head.

Next moment she slammed into him and, caught off his guard, they fell to the ground. Then she flung herself on top of him, filling his nostrils with the smell of strong soap and middle-aged woman.

An instant later the strange object struck the earth some 200 yards away. The ground heaved and trembled violently like a live thing. Something smacked him violently in the face. Then he blacked out.

He awoke with half a dozen anxious faces staring down at him, as the woman who had jumped on top of him brought across a steaming cup of tea. "*Stoi?*" he began in Russian and then remembering where he was asked in a slight daze, "What happened?"

"Buzz-bomb," the woman with the tea said in an exaggerated fashion, as if she were talking to an idiot. "It . . . was . . . a buzz-bomb, Ruskie."

"What's a buzz-bomb?" he asked and sat up. Immediately the middle-aged woman put the cup of hot tea to his lips, with "Plenty of sugar in it! Takes you out of shock."

"The V1," another of the middle-aged wardens said, eyes behind his horn-rimmed spectacles looking worried as he gazed at the Russian naval officer.

"*Da, ponemayu,*" he said. "I understand. I have read of them in the *Pravda.*"

"He speaks English just like what we do," the woman with the tea said, as if it were a great achievement.

Now he understood why there had been no car for him and why the forecourt to the airfield had been deserted. He had walked straight into an air-raid, an attack by these robot-planes that Hitler had been firing at London since the previous summer. "Thank you . . . thank you very much!" he said, smiling around at their fat, concerned faces. "You are very kind to me." He took the tea gently from the woman. "Very good tea. Just like in Russia."

"Char's good for everything," the warden with the glasses said encouragingly.

'Char?' he queried. Then he remembered the Russia "*chai*". Obviously it was the word some English used for tea. "Good for everything," he echoed and the English people looked happy and nodded to each other, as if everything was now all right.

"Have a smoke," one of the wardens said. "It's only a gasper, but it'll settle yer nerves, old pal."

Gratefully he accepted the lit cigarette and puffed at it happily, savouring the rich taste of the tobacco after the Russian *marhaka*, the black tobacco wrapped in newspaper, which he usually smoked, telling himself what kind people these English were.

"How's Uncle Joe?" the woman asked after a while.

"*Uncle Joe?*" he queried, puzzled, as he finished off the last of his 'char'.

"Joe ... Joe Stalin," the man with the glasses prompted.

"Is that what you call him, Uncle Joe?"

They nodded, smiling at him encouragingly, as one might at a child who was being asked to perform or recite a poem.

"*Uncle Joe,*" he muttered under his breath. "*Boshe moi.*" Didn't they know what a monster the dictator was? Aloud he said, trying to smile, "Well, he doesn't invite me for – er – *char* often!"

They laughed at that.

"But I hear he's well."

"Ay," the one with glasses said stoutly, "he's winning the damned war for us, I can tell you that. We and the Yanks have never done enough, like you Ruskies have. We should have got stuck in in 1942. Second front now sort of stuff." He froze suddenly. The sirens had started to wail dolefully once more. To the south-east the anti-aircraft guns began banging away. "Here the buggers come again!" the man with the glasses exclaimed. "There's no end to the sods." He turned to Sarov. "Pardon my French, please. But it gets right on my tits."

The woman who had jumped on Sarov scowled and then they were all putting their helmets back on and the young Russian naval officer realised that he was superfluous. Yet all the same he felt a warm glow of comradeship, even friendship for these first English men and women he had ever met. From his studies before the war he had always thought the English were very rich, aristocratic people or crushingly poor and exploited as they were in the novels by Charles Dickens. But these English people weren't like that at all.

Suddenly he remembered why he was here in London and he frowned. It was going to be his task to deprive these kind, ordinary people of their leader. It wasn't a pleasant thought.

Four hours later he was in a packed train from King's Cross, heading north for Hull. In one pocket he had a thick wad of English £5 notes; in the other he had a pistol, complete with silencer. As Igor had told him during the quick briefing at the embassy, "Comrade Commander, there must be absolutely no connection between us and what is to happen to this Commander Fleming of theirs. The pistol is English. If the assassin is taken, the money found on him will be English, too, drawn from a dozen different banks in London so it can't be traced to us.

Once Fleming is dealt with, then the way is open for the Fritzes to do what they want with the plutocrat Churchill."

He grinned showing his perfect set of stainless steel teeth. "Mind you, I, for one, shall miss the nice soft decadent life of London. The English know how to live." He had touched his fingers to his lips, "And their women! How different they are to those fat *babuskas* we have back home! Yes, I shall miss London." He had sighed and given Sarov a cynical grin.

As the train crowded with servicemen, some sleeping in the corridors, others in the luggage nets above the seats, even asleep in the toilets, rolled northward through the flat English countryside, Sarov remembered the briefing. Igor was like the rest of them, Beria and his toadies. They didn't really believe in Russia or communism, he told himself. They were time-servers, concerned only with their own positions and pleasures, perverted or otherwise. And he was being used to further their little schemes. In the end, he would become like they were, he knew that instinctively. He frowned even harder.

The little man in the blue suit was waiting for him at Paragon Street Station, as arranged by Igor. He recognised the Russian naval uniform immediately and walked straight up to Sarov. Touching his hand to his shabby cap in mock servility, he said, "Commander Sarov?"

The Russian looked down at him, hardly able to conceal his contempt. "Yes."

"Let me take your attaché case, sir," the little man said and then coming closer as he took the case, he whispered, "I've got your man, sir. Sailor on the trot. Do anything for money."

"On the trot?" Sarov asked, puzzled, as they started

to push their way through the throng towards the exit.

"Deserter, sir," the little man explained. "Been on the run for two years now. Done all sorts of jobs to keep going. Lives with a tart somewhere in James Street. Wouldn't be surprised if he ain't croaked somebody already."

The Russian had understood only half of what the servile little man, with his crooked grin and his sly eyes, was saying. But he knew instinctively he was a rogue who would probably sell his own mother for a handful of kopecks.

Suddenly it came to him. By a sheer effort of will he kept walking so that the little man didn't notice anything. Otherwise he would have stopped, overcome by the shock of this great revelation. Here, in England, he, Sarov, was free. There was no secret police to force him to do anything he didn't want to do. Beria was over 1000 kilometres away. Here he could make any decision he liked without fear. Abruptly he felt light-headed, as if he had just drunk 100 grams of pepper vodka. HE WAS FREE!

Chapter Five

"I expect you here been whoring around again," Fleming said gruffily, menacingly slapping his open palm with the leather dog whip. "You know I've forbidden you to do so while you're with me. You understand that, eh? Still you do it." He looked at the big whore menacingly. "Naturally, you know you'll have to be punished for it."

The big whore played the little game the toff liked. After all he was giving her two big white ones per session now. That was more than she could earn for a couple of long nights in the streets. She hung her head and said, "I'm sorry, sir."

"You damn well ought to be," Fleming snapped. "Now off with that skirt!"

"Knickers, too, sir?"

"Not yet. Keep them on for the time being until I tell you to take them off. Just depends on how you take your punishment, and you *deserve* it!"

"I know I do, sir," she said tamely. She started to undo her skirt, with her broad back to him. In the dressing table mirror she caught a glimpse of her own face. She winked at herself knowingly and under her breath she muttered, "Silly toffee-nosed bugger. He'll have to put on some more muscle to hurt Rosie Lee!"

She dropped her skirt and stepped out of it to reveal

that her firm, large buttocks were clad in sheer black silk knickers.

Fleming licked his lips greedily. "I say," he said thickly. "That's a splendid pair of knickers!"

"I put them on especially to please you, sir," she said meekly. "I know you like me in nice underthings."

"Yes, of course. But that doesn't mean you can escape your just punishment." He slapped the dog whip against his open palm suggestively.

"I understand, sir."

"Now, bend over the back of that armchair, and be quick about it! I'm getting impatient. I've not got all day, you know!"

She bent over the back of the old leather chair, her buttocks raised in the air so that the thin black silk was stretched even tighter to reveal every contour of her large rump.

Fleming's eyes glittered. He was getting very sexually aroused.

Somehow she sensed it. She could see that now familiar look in his long face. She raised her rump even more, hoping that the more aroused he was the sooner this stupid – and painful – game would be over. He raised the dog whip. "Now then, I don't want a lot of noise! You'll just have to grin and bear it. Take your medicine!" He breathed in hard and prepared to bring the lash down on those tremendous black-clad buttocks. But on this particular evening Commander Fleming was not fated to enjoy his perverse pleasures. For at that moment, the phone next to the bed started to ring.

"Damn and blast!" he cursed, the whip still raised. For a moment he was tempted not to pick the thing up. But then he realised it would have to be done. This was a duty call. None of his friends in London knew he was in

Hull. Admiral Godfrey, the head of Naval Intelligence, had ordered him to keep his visit to the northern port secret for the sake of security. "Remain where you are," he ordered the whore, still bent over the armchair. "Don't make a move or it will be the worse for you."

"Yes sir," she answered dutifully and under her breath muttered, "Silly daft bugger. Why can't he just stick it in me like a normal bloke."

Angrily, Fleming snatched the phone from the cradle and barked, "Fleming!"

"Commander," Howling Mad snapped back, "there's been an amazing development!" He sounded very excited.

"What? How do you mean?"

On the armchair the big whore relaxed. Somehow she guessed there was going to be no sex this evening. She straightened up and reached for her skirt. He nodded his permission and dropped the dog whip.

"Are you alone?" Howling Mad queried.

"I will be in a minute." With a jerk of his head Fleming indicated the whore should take her coat and go.

She did so quickly. She had the money and she had done nothing for it. That suited her fine.

Fleming waited till she had closed the door, then he said: "Well, what has happened, Commander?"

"I won't tell you the details over the phone, Fleming. Not secure enough. But now we've got something definite. I suggest that you come over here P.D.Q."

"Pretty damned quick it is then, Commander," Fleming answered. As he put down the phone he gave the dog whip a hearty kick and sent it flying under the bed, where it collided with the tin chamberpot. There was going to be no sex for him this evening, that was obvious.

Sarov rose hastily as Fleming came in and bowed stiffly from the waist then extended his hand. "Sarov," he announced.

Slightly bewildered, Fleming took the hand and shook it. He noted to his surprise that the pale-faced blond young man was wearing Russian naval uniform underneath a civilian coat.

Howling Mad made the introductions and said, as O'Rourke guarded the door with a service pistol holstered to the belt around his waist, "Commander Sarov has been sent here as an assistant Russian naval attaché. He reported to the police two hours ago and said he didn't want to return to London. The police contacted Special Branch, who ordered Commander Sarov to be brought here. They think our station is the most secure place in Hull."

Fleming looked slightly bewildered at the sudden flow of information. All the same, he felt a growing sense of excitement. They were on to something at last, he knew it.

Howling Mad produced a bottle of scotch from inside his desk and poured them all a drink. The pale-faced Russian looked relieved. It was obvious he needed a drink. Howling Mad raised his glass. "Down the hatch," he said.

The Russian raised his glass to his chest, elbow set at a 45 degree angle and barked, "*Nastrovya*". To the others' amazement he downed the half tumbler of fiery spirits in one gulp.

"Well," Fleming said after a sip. "What's the story?"

Howling Mad actually smiled, "*You're* the story, Fleming."

"What?"

Howling Mad nodded to the young Russian. "Tell him, Commander."

Sarov hesitated, but now he knew he was safe, there was no need for him to hold anything back. "Commander Fleming, I was sent from Moscow to arrange your murder."

Fleming nearly dropped his glass. *What did you say?*"

Sarov repeated it and an astonished Fleming asked, "But why . . . Why me?"

Sarov didn't hesitate, "Because our secret police think you know too much. Therefore it would be better if you were put out of the way."

"Know too much . . . put out of the way?"

Guarding the door O'Rourke was amused at the way Fleming was stuttering. He had certainly lost his Etonian calm this time.

Sarov looked at the bottle of scotch. Howling Mad understood, reached out and poured the young Russian another hefty swig. Sarov smiled his thanks. "Our people. No, I say it different," he corrected himself, his face suddenly bitter. "*Their* people, the people who oppress us and hurt us." He realised his English was becoming more fluent by the hour, and went on, "They want you dealt with because they think you and your friends," he indicated Howling Mad and O'Rourke, who had taken to the obviously sincere Russian, wearing his heart on his sleeve in a manner that no Englishman could, "are finding out too much."

"About what?" Fleming asked.

This time it was Howling Mad who answered. "About the *Tirpitz* and Mr Churchill."

At the door O'Rourke tensed. He asked himself the

question that Fleming posed aloud the next moment, "What's the connection with the German battleship and old Winnie Churchill?"

Sarov drained his whisky in that bold, determined manner of his. He said, "I don't know the actual connection." He licked his lips, as if they were suddenly dry. "But there is one. But I shall tell you this, comrades."

The three British naval officers were a bit startled at his use of the term 'comrades', but they said nothing. "Go on," Howling Mad said encouragingly, filling the Russian's glass for the third time. Commander Keith was not a very sensitive man, but he felt the young Russian needed as much strong drink as he could stand. It wasn't every day that a Russian naval officer deserted his country for a very uncertain future.

"Old Leather Face, the dictator Stalin to you, wants not only you killed, Commander Fleming, but he also wants to have your Mr Churchill liquidated."

"Christ!" Fleming exclaimed. "Whatever for?"

"Very simple," Sarov answered and drained his glass for yet a third time. "Because your Prime Minister stands in the way of his plans for post-war Europe."

Fleming whistled softly and Howling Mad exclaimed, "Fine bunch of Allies we've got. First the Yanks, and now the Ruskies – er – Russians planning to murder the PM." He looked puzzled. "But I can't yet see the connection. How can your Uncle Joe – Stalin – get the Germans, in the shape of the *Tirpitz*, to work for him?"

Sarov shrugged a little helplessly. "That is a question I can't answer, Commander. I do not know the circumstances here in England. All I know is that your Mr Churchill has been in Russia, at a place called Yalta, on the Crimean Sea, for a week. When he comes back to this country, the Germans will attempt to liquidate him. You, or so I have learned in Moscow, were getting close to finding out what the Fritzes' plan was. For that reason," he nodded at Fleming, who had lost all thoughts of sex now that he knew that he was the target for a Russian murder plan, "Commander Fleming here had to be eliminated. By the time, or so I was told, you were back to finding out what the Fritzes were going to do to Mr Churchill, it would be too late."

Silence descended upon the office as the four officers considered the situation. Outside, a drunken matelot staggering home presumably from the local Hedon Road pubs was singing off-key. His voice died away in the distance.

"All right," Fleming said slowly and carefully, "the Hun has raised and re-commissioned the *Tirpitz*. We haven't got a ship on this side of the globe to stop her. According to you, Commander Keith, due to the weather conditions at this time of the year in the Channel and North Sea the RAF would be pretty useless as well. So presumably the *Tirpitz* could do just what it bloody well liked in our waters."

Howling Mad nodded and said, "Agreed," while Sarov looked longingly at the bottle of whisky.

"So what can the *Tirpitz* have to do with bunping off old Winnie Churchill?" Fleming mused. "The battleship can't sail up the Thames to the Houses of Parliament to do the old man in like van Tromp tried to do back in the 17th century, can she?"

"But perhaps Mr Churchill might not be in London?" Sarov suggested. "Perhaps—" He never ended his suggestion.

Suddenly the window shattered. Something round and hard and metallic clattered on to the floor of the room.

O'Rourke, the youngest there, reacted immediately. *"Duck!"* he yelled. *"Grenade!"*

Howling Mad fell behind his desk. Fleming dropped to the floor. But the Russian was too slow. Perhaps it was the drink. Perhaps he hadn't understood the warning in English. The grenade exploded in a flash of ugly red light as shrapnel hissed outwards and upwards. It tore at his upright body, ripping at the flesh, gashing and bloodying him. He moaned piteously then slowly sank to the floor, dead already before he got there.

Chapter Six

Shocked and still deafened by the explosion at such close quarters, the other three had their cuts attended to by the medics as the corpse was borne out, the blood dripping through the canvas of the brown stretcher.

Special Branch and the police were on their way. "Poor devil!" Howling Mad commented as the RAMC man bandaged a deep shrapnel cut on his brawny upper arm. "But one thing is clear." He looked at the pool of blood in the centre of the floor. "He was speaking the truth. Why this, otherwise?"

Fleming, white faced with shock and hands trembling, after nearly six years of war had never seen any action like the other two had, said, "You're right, Commander Keith. This bears it out. They were desperate to kill him before he told us all he knew."

O'Rourke, who had a plaster stuck over a nasty gash on his forehead, said, "I think, sir, he *did* tell us all he knew. We don't know, of course, who his associates are here in Hull. We don't know, too, how they knew about you, Commander Fleming."

Fleming blushed. Suddenly it came to him with the instant understanding of a revelation. It was the pimp and the big whore. They were the two who knew all about his movements in the Northern port. They were types who could be bought easily because he had thought he'd bought them himself. He knew he had been tricked. Somehow he couldn't visualise the little pimp doing the killing himself, but he could have easily bought someone to do the job for him. For the time being he kept that knowledge to himself.

Aloud, Fleming said, "So let's sum this up. Stalin wants Churchill bumped off for political reasons, but he's going to let the Huns do the job for him. Naturally he doesn't want to be involved directly. We haven't won the war yet and he still wants Anglo-American co-operation and help. The Hun plot to kill Churchill clearly involves the *Tirpitz*." He frowned and paused for a moment. "The overwhelming question is," he said after a moment or two, "how in heaven's name is the *Tirpitz* going to get at old Winnie?"

Howling Mad said, "Well, as we now know Churchill's in Russia. Will he be coming back after his conference there by ship? Would the *Tirpitz* try to tackle that ship in the Med?"

Fleming considered for a few seconds, then said, "Hardly likely, don't you think? There'd be the long haul along the French coast, which is mostly in our hands now. There'd also be the running the gauntlet of the Channel and the straits at Gib. Too many things could go wrong in a sea journey of that kind. No, not the Med, I feel."

Again silence descended upon the shattered office, as bells outside indicated that a police car was on its way to investigate the bombing

"May I say something, sir?" O'Rourke ventured.

"Fire away, O'Rourke," Howling Mad snapped. He had obviously already overcome his shock at the sudden attack.

"Well, sir, can't we find out Mr Churchill's movements

and work from what we know about them? See if we can spot any connections?"

Howling Mad looked at Fleming. "You know about such things, Commander," he said. "What do you think?"

Fleming considered before saying carefully, "Well, Churchill isn't like President Roosevelt, you know, always accompanied by carloads of bodyguards carrying tommy-guns. The old boy has got only one bodyguard, Inspector Thompson, a fine chap from the London Met. But the Cabinet Office does keep his movements fairly secret, just in case. However, I think we could find out about his plans for the near future if we went through proper channels. Might take time though."

"Well, Commander Fleming," Howling Mad snorted, "I think you ought to get on to it. We can't go losing old Winnie now when he's virtually won the war for us."

On any other occasion O'Rourke would have laughed at the way his chief put it – 'losing old Winnie' – but after what had just happened he didn't feel like laughing. The situation was far too serious. He looked from Howling Mad to Fleming, whose hands, he noticed, were still shaking.

Fleming nodded. "You're right, Commander." He flashed a glance at his watch. "I've still got time to catch the midnight train to London. I expect I could get there by about eight tomorrow morning. Then I could see if my chief could work the oracle with the Cabinet Office."

"Make it ten o'clock, sir," O'Rourke corrected him. "It'll take at least ten hours to reach the capital. These days the east coast trains stop at every tinpot little station to let off troops and the like."

"Suppose you're right," Fleming agreed as he reached

139

for his cap, which was now looking decidedly battered by the explosion.

"Doesn't matter much," Howling Mad said with a malicious grin. "Those London Johnnies never start before ten as it is, war or no war."

"I'll rustle up a car for you, sir," O'Rourke said hastily. He knew Howling Mad once he got started on the hated and detested 'London Johnnies', who sat "on their fat behinds shuffling papers and ogling their secretaries' bottoms while we do the ruddy fighting," as Commander Keith always snorted.

"Thank you, O'Rourke," Fleming said, adding to Keith, "I'll inform you immediately I find out something which shows some sort of connection between Winnie and the *Tirpitz*." There was a knock at the door. "That'll be the flat-foots, what."

"Very probably. All right, Fleming, you cut along. I'll deal with the gentlemen in blue . . ."

Fleming reached the Admiralty building just as the sirens started to wail the 'All clear'. His chief Admiral Godfrey, was waiting for him. "Bloody V2 came down in Chiswick," he said. "Made one hell of a mess. The Hun responsible for those bloody things will have to be strung up next to Hitler after we've won the war, Ian."

"Man named Werner von Braun," Fleming answered a little wearily. "He's the inventor."

The big bluff Admiral looked at his subordinate warily. "You know a lot of things, Ian. Sometimes you surprise me, my boy. You might even make a success of those penny-dreadfuls you tell me you intend to write when you're demobbed." His manner changed. "All right, to business. I've called the Cabinet Office, pulled a few strings and all that. The PM's private secretary, a young chap called John Colville, has promised to come over in half an hour to brief you on Winnie's movements for the next month. Ex-fighter pilot with the RAF. Seems a nice sort of a bloke, for a politician," he added with a wink. "All right, Ian, go and get yourself tarted up. A wash and shave and see if someone can lend you a cap. That one looks as if it's been through the wars."

"It has, sir," Fleming said with feeling, but he didn't enlighten his chief with any more explanations; that would have been too complicated and perhaps embarrassing. Suddenly he remembered the dog whip that was still under the bed of the room he had used in Hull's Station Hotel. "Bollocks!" he cursed to himself and wondered what the chambermaid would make of that when she found it.

Colville was suave but businesslike. He took over and even Fleming realised that he was in the hands of a person who was at the centre of power, so he didn't ask too many questions. Instead he listened. "All right," Colville began. "You must realise to keep it under you hat."

Fleming nodded his agreement. As yet he had not told Churchill's private secretary the reason for his interest. He would do so afterwards.

Colville opened the little book he had brought with him and ran his elegantly manicured fingernail down the entries. "Tuesday, February 20th," he commenced. "The PM will atend the House for Questions." He looked at Fleming, as if he expected some response. Fleming gave none.

"Wednesday, February 21st. The PM will receive General Anders, commanding the Polish Corps in Italy. Something to do with the Yalta Conference, I expect."

Again Fleming's sulky face showed no reaction.

Colville continued with, "Thursday, February 22nd, blank. The PM has no official business on that day, it appears. The day after, we drive down to Chequers. There the PM is to draft a speech he'll give on the following Tuesday." He looked up at the Intelligence officer. Fleming showed no interest.

Colville grunted and looked down at the notebook again. "Friday, February 23rd," he continued, "we receive Bomber Harris – you know, Sir Arthur Harris. The PM wants to know his opinion of the effects of the raid on Dresden on the 14th. Saturday, the PM has lunch with President Benes of Czechoslovakia. That night we take the train north—"

"*What?*" Fleming's eyes flashed. "North? To where?"

Colville looked a little surprised by Fleming's sudden urgent interest. "Well, you know that the Home Guard is going to be stood down this month? There's going to be a big parade in London for them. The King is going to take the salute with several Home Counties battalions."

Fleming was already remembering what the Home Guards in charge of the German *Feldwebel* had been saying and the workers in Hull putting up the saluting stand.

"So the PM has decided he'd honour the North with something similar. After all he hasn't been to that part of the world since 1940 when he went up to Hornsea." Colville smiled at the memory. "Perhaps you remember that picture they took of him at the time, with a tommy-gun tucked under the arm and smoking a big cigar? He looked like Edward G. Robinson in one of those thirties' gangster pictures—"

"*Where?*" Fleming demanded brutally.

Colville looked displeased. "You mean where he's

going to take the Home Guard standing down parade salute?" he said very haughtily. Mere naval commanders didn't talk to him like that.

"Yes."

Colville looked at the notebook once more. "Why," he said, "he thought he'd pick a place that has suffered in the raids as much as London. And that city certainly has had enough of them. So far, 3,000 of them by the last count, I believe—"

"*Where*?"

"Hull," Colville answered.

Fleming breathed out hard. "Christ! We've got it!" he whispered, as if he were speaking to himself.

"Got what?"

Fleming didn't answer, he was no longer listening. While Colville watched, puzzled and not a little angry, he reached for the phone and said urgently, "Please place on urgent call through to Commander Keith of 15 Motor Torpedo Flotilla, based at Hull."

PART FOUR

Sink the *Tirpitz!*

Chapter One

"Now I'm shittingly well gonna sing," the nearly naked whore announced, "whether you Germans like it or not!"

The drunken sailors clapped and whistled, though they could hardly see her in the smoke-filled room. There were drunks sprawled out everywhere in pools of stale beer. A petty officer was hanging from a hatstand by his braces. In the corridor outside, a naked leading rating, with a herring stuck up his anus, was running back and forth crying, "Watch out for me, or I'll bite yer! *I'm a shark!*"

Staggering dangerously, dressed solely in somebody's seaboots and sheer red silk panties, she pushed her way through the drunken officers of the *Tirpitz*, fending off their hands as they tried to grab her buttocks.

"Get a load of the rigging she's got on her!" someone chortled. "I could climb up and down those tits all day long – even in a force ten gale."

The sally was greeted by a loud burst of laughter.

"Mind you, that kind of tackle could be used for better purposes than singing."

More laughter, for on nights like this when the crews got drunk at the expense of the 'Big Lion', Grand Admiral Doenitz, and knew at the back of their minds that perhaps they wouldn't come back, everything and anything was considered uproariously funny.

The Dutch whore, one of the several score who had been brought over from the mainland to the island of Texel for this special occasion, took a swig out of one of their beer glasses, shook her head as if slightly puzzled, then taking a vase of carnations threw them out and bending over the vase urinated in it with a loud gushing noise, the hot steam wreathing her dark thatch.

"More!" they cried . . . "*More!*"

Again she swayed dangerously, her eyes almost crossed and slurring her words, she muttered, "Ain't got as much piss in me as you *Moffen*." She meant Germans.

The whore staggered to the microphone, dragging a hardback chair with her. Very unsteadily she placed it next to the mike and propped one leg on the chair so that the audience could see the dyed black thatch and the pink slit beyond. There were shrill whistles and cries of "My God I'd like to get my tongue between those lips!"

The Dutch whore looked at the young officers contemptuously, as she accepted a lit cigarette from one of the naval band. "Yer," she sneered, "that's about all you *Moffen* can do. Make love with yer tongues like the frogs."

Again they whistled and cheered. They loved it.

"Yer've lost of course." She didn't specify what, but they knew what she meant. "But you're young men and I think you ought to have your pleasure, before it's all over." She turned and slowly gyrated her bottom so that they got a good view of the hard, tight globes of her buttocks. "Anyway – everywhere – every way!"

They knew what she meant and they clapped uproariously.

"When I'm a grandma," she went on, "with a cunt

made of leather, cos my real one wore out due to all the men who fucked it, I'll perhaps remember you. I'm not promising nothing," she admonished them, "mind you. But I just might. All the dead young *Moffen*." She looked around their excited, flushed faces, as if she were seriously trying to etch their features on her mind's eye! And. "I'll wonder what you died for." She sprang to attention and, almost falling from the little stage, thrust out her right arm in the Hitler salute, crying, "For *Volk, Vaterland and Führer*, perhaps." She sneered a second later. "You did it for whores without knickers, who were pissed like a thousand men." (She used the German expression.)" "For whores who showed yer their beavers. For whores who did things for yer that those nice, fat Frauleins back home wouldn't do. You know." She pursed her lips and sucked the end of the microphone.

The young officers went wild. One started to rip open his flies, crying, "I don't care if they put me in the pox hospital for the rest of my born days, but I'm going to have a slice of that!" It was only with difficulty that his comrades restrained him and made him sit down.

Sitting next to Captain Hartmann, the captain of the *Tirpitz*, his second-in-command, *Kapitanleutnant* Dietz snorted, "I say that's going a bit too far, even for a place like this. That whore is insulting everything we Germans stand for." He began to rise.

Hartmann tugged at his arm and said, "Sit down, Dietz. They don't feel insulted. They're too young, perhaps, to understand that they are being insulted. Besides they're fascinated by her."

On the little stage the drunken whore relaxed a little. She announced, "Now I'm going to sing. You all know the song. Most of you have been singing it since 1939." Again she looked at the drunken, flushed young officers contemptuously and sneered, "The only thing is you never got there – and never will now." She raised her voice and nodded to the little orchestra. "Right, here we go, *Wir fahren gegen England*." It was the marching song of the German Navy – 'we're sailing to England'.

There was a tremendous roar from the audience. They were not one bit insulted by the whore's remarks. Now they joined in the chorus of that old marching song, "*Kommt die Kunde du bist gefallen . . .*"

Hartmann allowed himself a little cynical smile while next to him Dietz flushed angrily. "Who knows, Number one," he remarked, "the whore might be wrong after all." He reached for his cap. "Come on, we don't want to inhibit them any longer. They'll be wanting to take off their uniforms soon and get stuck into the whores. It'll be their last chance to let their hair down and they know it."

Dietz took his gold-braid cap too and said, "I can't get out of the place soon enough, *Herr Kapitan!*"

At the opposite table a young lieutenant, more sober than the rest, saw that the skipper was leaving. He rose to his feet and was about to order the rest to attention as a sign of respect. Gently Hartmann shook his head and the young officer sat down again hastily.

They closed the blackout curtains behind them and went out into the freezingly cold night. For a while they walked in silence down the deserted cobbled road of the little town. Behind them the roar of scores of young voices bellowing out the old marching song died away. Now there was no sound save the lap-lap of the waves against the quay.

Finally Hartmann broke the heavy silence with, "It's Saturday 24th February."

"What, sir?" Dietz said a little startled, as if he had been thinking of other things.

"We carry out the operation on Saturday February 24th," Hartmann repeated. "Doenitz called me just before the social evening started. The date was given to him by our listening and de-coding service."

"That means we start on the Friday?"

"Exactly, and fortunately we'll have darkness with us most of the way. Naturally we'll be given some air cover once it grows light on the Saturday. We shall also have an escort of some surface craft. There'll also be a decoy on a course for Norway. Naturally both the decoy and the *Tirpitz* will be picked up by the Tommies' radar. But it will mean they'll have to divide their resources to check the two of us."

Dietz stopped abruptly, his face looking very excited in the cold spectral light cast by the half moon above the island. "Heaven, arse and cloudburst! If we pull this one off it'll change the course of history! Get rid of Churchill and—" He stopped short, he could see that the skipper didn't share his enthusiasm. "Anything wrong, sir?" he ended a little lamely.

Hartmann hesitated. He knew Dietz was a patriotic German, but no Nazi. Still, ever since the attempt on Hitler's life the previous July, one had to be very careful about what one said. There were people everywhere ready to denounce you to the Gestapo; and that meant a swift trial in the People's Court and a slow death hanging from a piece of chicken wire. All the same, Dietz was a professional naval officer and seaman, who needed to know what his skipper thought about the great operation to come. Slowly *Kapitan* Hartmann started to explain.

"You know, Dietz, that whore back there was right.

Those young men already bear the mark of Cain on them."

"I don't understand exactly, sir," Dietz said in a puzzled tone.

"Well, look at it like this. They'll kill, if we strike lucky, but they will be killed in their turn. I looked at them back there and I must admit that tears came to my eyes as I did so. They are all roughly the same age as my boy, Karl-Heinz, was when—" He didn't finish, but Dietz knew what he was talking about. The skipper's boy had been third officer in a U-boat which had disappeared in the Channel just after the Invasion. But he said nothing.

"Now the whore lets them see her beaver and mouths a few obscenities. With that and the drink and, if they're lucky later, a little bit of the two-backed bears dancing the mattress polka, that will have been their lives. Not much really," he added in an almost matter-of-fact tone.

"Yes, I suppose, sir, that some of them will have to die, but they'll die *gladly* for Germany. Ever since this war started they have learned to die willingly for the Fatherland!"

"I wish they could learn to *live* for the Fatherland," Hartmann said quietly, his face hollowed out to a death's head in the cold hard light of the moon.

"Some will survive."

"Will they?" Hartmann asked. "If we are successful in this operation, do you think the Tommies will let us get away with it?"

"I, for one, am confident," Dietz replied stoutly.

"I'm not! I'm as good a German as anyone and I shall do my duty as is expected of me. I wouldn't have got the job if Doenitz had not had the fullest confidence in my ability to carry out my task to the best of my abilities."

He hesitated, his voice very thoughful. "But imagine what the British reaction will be if we do succeed? They will hound us relentlessly. Somehow or other they'll send the *Tirpitz* to the bottom, Dietz," he concluded, staring hard at his Number One as if seeing him for the very first time. "We're doomed – the lot of us." Then Captain Hartmann chuckled, "Come on, let's get back to the billets and have one last glass of that good Dutch *genever* to erase these gloomy thoughts, eh."

Together they started walking rapidly down the deserted street, almost as if they were being chased.

Chapter Two

Churchill sat in the tub of hot water looking like a pink and plump cherub. His false teeth were in a glass to one side of him. At the other side there was another glass containing brandy. As he washed himself he puffed at a big cigar almost happily.

"Not exactly the usual gentleman's early morning bath," Colville told himself slightly amused at the sight. "Brandy and cigars at eight in the morning!"

"Well, John," Churchill mumbled, the usual growl absent due to his lack of teeth, "what brings the day?"

Colville opened his notebook and read out the list of minor appointments which he had arranged for the Prime Minister, who had no time to remember the details of trivia. "The main thing is, of course, Questions in the House at two this afternoon, Prime Minister."

"Yes, yes," Churchill said, waving the cigar as if it were a spear. "I recall that. I suppose those dreadful Labour people will be expecting me to make a lot of complimentary statements about Uncle Joe," he emphasised the term contemptuously, "and what a misnomer that is. I have never seen anyone less avuncular. That man has more blood on his hands than Caligula."

Colville waited politely for him to finish before saying, "A problem has been brought to my attention, Prime Minister."

"*A problem has been brought to my attention*," Churchill mimicked the tone savagely. "Now that seems to me to be very civil service, John!"

Colville felt himself blushing. But Churchill, who never considered other people's feelings, paid no attention. Indeed, Colville felt that in that aristocratic manner of his Churchill didn't even notice. "Well, fire away then. What is it?"

"I've been talking to a Commander Fleming of Naval Intelligence—"

"Is there such a thing?" Churchill cut in sarcastically.

Colville thought it better to ignore the comment. He continued with, "He fears that an attempt might be made on your life."

Churchill took the news calmly. "John," he said, "ever since I was an 18-year-old straight out of Harrow attempts have been made on my life. I am quite used to the fact that I live and have lived dangerously for most of my years. But pray go on."

As best he could, Colville explained about the proposed attempt on Fleming's life and the Russian dissident who had been killed by an unknown assassin, while Churchill listened quietly, smoking his big cigar and occasionally splashing some water over his fat, hairless body.

When Colville was finished, he said softly, "So Stalin has knowledge of a German plan to assassinate me and is actively supporting the plan in an indirect manner. Is that what you mean, John?"

"Yes sir," Colville agreed as Churchill, dripping water, rose from the bath to finish his brandy.

"Please hand me the towel."

Colville did so and after Churchill was dry he put on his silk vest which did not cover his lower body. But

Churchill, in that aristocratic manner of his, had never been ashamed of running round half naked.

"So what does this Commander – er – Fleming wish me to do, pray?" Churchill asked.

"I've got him outside. Perhaps he ought to tell you himself, Prime Minister."

"All right then," Churchill agreed. "But do hand me the glass with my false teeth." He flashed Colville a toothless smile. "I must have my teeth in. You see, although you might not think so I do have my little vanities, John!"

Colville did as he was ordered, telling himself that the PM was a cunning old dog. He appeared to be oblivious to all about him. Yet at the same time he noted everything.

A few moments later Fleming was ushered into the dressing-room next door to find the Prime Minister of Britain, the most important man in the whole of the British Empire, being helped into somewhat long and baggy silken underpants by a man servant. That completed, Churchill waved the servant away and pulled on his own trousers. "Chap's got to learn look after himself," he said to no one in particular. "The next time we have an election, I might be out on my neck and all this," he waved his hand vaguely around the room, "will have vanished."

"The electorate wouldn't do that, sir," Fleming felt compelled to say. "Not after what you have done for this country since 1940."

"A fickle people, the English," Churchill growled. "Good but fickle.

"Now then, my dear Commander, tell me the dreadful prediction," Churchill smiled so that in a way Fleming felt an absolute fool, as if what he would have to say was really of no importance whatsoever.

Hastily, stumbling a little over the words, Fleming told

the Premier what he knew, while the latter continued to dress until finally Churchill asked, "And what would you have me do, Fleming?"

"Well obviously, sir, we don't know all the details, but we think you're in grave danger. We suggest you cancel your visit to Hull. That would be the simplest solution."

Churchill's winning smile vanished. "*Cancel!*" he echoed as if shocked. "Cancel a visit to those brave people who have suffered so much since 1941, when Hull became the main port of supply for our convoys to Russia? Do you think those 10,000 merchant seamen who lost their lives on the Murmansk run could cancel? Or all those thousands of middle-aged men who answered Mr Eden's call to set up the Home Guard and who have spent years guarding the coast and the Humber eastuary up there against a German invasion could cancel?" Churchill's eyes blazed and now he sounded as as if he were addressing the floor of the House of Commons on some great national issue. "They deserve my presence up there. They shall have it, too." He lowered his voice to a more normal level, as he struggled into his waistcoat and placed his watch and chain in the lower pockets.

"Besides, don't you realise, Commander, this is also a great opportunity for us. We have been trying to sink the *Tirpitz* for years. We thought we had done it last November. Apparently the job wasn't done well enough. Now, whatever role she is to play in my supposed assassination, we'll have her in the open. It will be a golden opportunity to rid ourselves of her for good."

Fleming didn't attempt to dissuade the stubborn old man with the arguments that Howling Mad Keith had offered him 48 hours before. After all Churchill had been the First Lord of the Admiralty back in 1939 when Fleming had first joined the 'Wavy Navy'. Churchill knew all about naval warfare. Instead he said, "What do you suggest, sir?"

Churchill looked hard at him. "Well, I am not accustomed, Commander Fleming, to dealing with the minutiae of military matters. I know, of course, that the *Tirpitz* is the greatest battleship afloat and that we have at the present time nothing to match her in the Home Fleet. I would suggest that, if you *do* believe in these fantasies dreamed up by Russian Jews and renegades, you take yourself back to Hull and plan what can be done once the *Tirpitz* takes to the sea."

"I see, sir."

Churchill could see the disappointment reflected upon Fleming's face and as he was not an unkind man, just an unfeeling one, he took Fleming by the arm as if they were old friends and said, "I shall walk you to the door of Number Ten, Commander Fleming. At least you can tell your chaps that the Prime Minister escorted you to the door."

Behind their backs Colville shook his head in mock wonder. As always the Prime Minister was completely unpredictable. But like the obedient servant he was he trotted after them. Perhaps the PM would need him down below.

In the entrance, a hard-faced man with an old-fashioned moustache was waiting. He was dressed somewhat sloppily, Fleming couldn't help thinking, in the uniform of an RAF Air Marshal. He straightened up a little when he saw Churchill with the young, elegant naval commander, but the grumpy sour look didn't vanish from his broad powerful face.

"Well, Sir Arthur," Churchill said, "what of Dresden?"

'Bomber Harris', for the Air Marshal was no less a person than the commander of Bomber Command, looked at the Prime Minister and then at the young naval officer, before replying, "Sir, there is no such place as Dresden."

Even Churchill looked surprised. "I say!" he exclaimed. "Did you say what I thought you did?"

Harris nodded, his face as dour as ever. "Yes, Prime Minister, we have razed Dresden from the face of the earth. Back in 1940 I remember standing on the roof of the Air Ministry building and watching London burn all around me. I told myself then that the Hun had sown the seed. Now he has reaped the whirlwind."

"Well put, Sir Arthur," Churchill said. "Well said indeed! Now then, this young fellah here tells me that the *Tirpitz* will soon be on the loose once more."

"Sunk her back in November in Altenfjord," Harris replied in that no-nonsense manner of his.

"Yes, of course. But the Hun has secretly raised and refitted her, it appears," Churchill replied.

"Never trust a Hun. What is it you once said yourself, sir? The Hun's either at your feet grovelling or at your throat trying to strangle you. What?"

Churchill chuckled. "I suppose I did say that once. But now a question, Sir Arthur. If the *Tirpitz* does go on the rampage, what can your chaps of Bomber Command do to stop her?"

Harris didn't even seem to consider. Bluntly he said, "*Nothing*! Not at this time of the year."

"Why at this time of the year?"

"Because of the weather conditions. At the height my Lancasters would have to fly to drop their Tallboys they wouldn't be able to see the target."

"What about air-to-ground radar, Sir Arthur?" Churchill queried.

"They are not yet fitted with it. Besides, out in the

open sea I don't think the radar sets would give the bomb-aimers the definition they would need to outline and pinpoint the *Tirpitz*."

Churchill absorbed the information, while Fleming studied the stocky Air Marshal with his bristling, old-fashioned moustache. As always he was storing information for future use. Harris would make an interesting character for one of his 'penny dreadfuls', as his chief, the Admiral, was wont to call the novels he planned to write.

"No," Harris snapped, "the only way I think you could sink the *Tirpitz* would be to use some sort of Kamikaze like the Japs are now using out in the Far East."

"*Kamikaze?*" the Prime Minister echoed.

"Yes, a suicide plane packed with high explosive. Damned Nips crash 'em right into our ships if they can. They might call me 'Butcher Harris' – behind my back, mind you – but I wouldn't let my chaps commit suicide like that. Lost enough of them already in normal aerial warfare."

"I quite understand, Sir Arthur," Churchill said soothingly.

He nodded to the butler, who opened the door to let Fleming out. "Well, Commander," he said cheerfully, apparently in no way affected by the news that Fleming had brought, "hie yourself back to Hull and see what's going on. Please keep me informed. Goodbye and good luck to you."

Fleming touched his hand to his cap in salute and told himself that for all his faults, Churchill was truly a great man. Then the door closed on his face and he was walking out of Downing Street. It was only when he turned the corner and had left the street behind him that it came to him. "*Kamikaze*," he said aloud. "*Kamikaze . . .*"

Chapter Three

Howling Mad, flanked by Fleming, looked around at his young skippers' faces. They were all bright, intelligent and eager. He knew that for them, mostly young men in their early twenties, the war was still an adventure, not the bloody violent business which it really was. Still, he liked what he saw.

"All right, gentlemen, you've heard what Commander Fleming has just said. Mr Churchill won't be put off. Stubborn old bulldog that he is, he is still coming to Hull although Commander Fleming warned him that his life might be at risk. So what can *we* do?" He answered his own question at once. "Coastal Command has been alerted and they are going to send out regular patrols when the weather is good." He nodded through the window at the thick white fog which curled around his HQ. "But today they are locked in by that damned fog and at this time of the year the same thing could happen every day."

He took a sip from the big glass of pink gin in front of him. It was only ten in the morning but when Howling Mad wanted a drink, he took one regardless of the time of day. "So we've got to take up the slack, gentlemen," he continued. "We must have patrols out in a 50-mile area off Spurn Point on a 24-hour basis. Whatever tricks the Hun will try to get

161

up with the *Tirpitz*, we must be prepared for them. Is that clear?"

There was a murmur of agreement.

Outside, in the Estuary, a foghorn wailed like the cry of some lost soul. O'Rourke shivered instinctively and asked, "But what exactly are we to look for, sir?" He knew he was chancing his luck with Howling Mad. Even now, with half a tumbler of strong gin inside him, he hadn't mellowed. His temper was needle-sharp.

"How the devil am I supposed to know, O'Rourke! If I knew I would have told you already, wouldn't I?" He spun round on Fleming. "Well, what do you think, Commander?"

Fleming took the affected ivory cigarette holder out of the side of his mouth and said slowly, "I've been giving the matter some consideration. It seems that the *Tirpitz* can now roam the North Sea with impunity. The RAF can't stop her. The Home Fleet, which is now virtually non-existent, as you all know, can't either. If that's the case what is the German plan? Is the *Tirpitz* going to play a role in the would-be assassination of the Prime Minister?" He let his words sink in for a few minutes.

Outside, a Party of ratings were marching through the fog back to their ship, the sound they made muffled by the white mist until the leading hand cried, "All right, me lucky lads, let's have a song to cheer us up a bit. What about '*Tight as a drum, never been done, queen of the all the fairies. Isn't it a pity she's only one titty to feed the baby on. Poor little bugger he's only one sucker . . .!*'"

For once, Howling Mad didn't blow up and start bellowing like a crazy man through the windows at the men. Perhaps he was too preoccupied with their problem.

"Perhaps," Fleming continued, the blue smoke wreathing its way around his broken-nosed face, "the

Hun will attempt to land a commando party, trained killers. I mean they pulled off that tremendous stunt in '43 when they rescued Mussolini from those Wops who had imprisoned him. And only last year they collared the son of the Hungarian dictator Horthy in an attempt to blackmail Hungary to stay in the war on Germany's side. We haven't got the monopoly on commando raids, you know."

"Please get on with it, Commander," Howling Mad said impatiently, as outside the sound of singing died away in the fog. "We haven't got all the time in the world."

"Of course, of course," Fleming pacified him. "But whatever the Huns are up to, we must stop them before they can start an operation against Churchill. We must knock the *Tirpitz* out."

"But that is impossible, sir," O'Rourke said. "Everybody says that."

Fleming was not offended by the interruption. Indeed it offered him the opportunity he wanted to display his own cleverness. "Agreed. But so far everyone has been talking about conventional methods of dealing with the *Tirpitz*: bombing by the RAF, gunfire from big ships, and so on. But there is another method."

"What?" Howling Mad demanded. Fleming was beginning to irritate him. The fellow was too clever by half.

"Kamikaze," Fleming said simply.

"What?"

Fleming repeated the Japanese word and added, "It's the Nip for 'Divine wind'."

"Well, I must say it gives me the wind when I read about those Nip buggers." He laughed at his own humour.

Nobody joined in and he stopped in mid-laugh, a sudden scowl on his broad, ruddy face.

"Well, we haven't got any Kamikaze pilots or so I have been reliably told by 'Bomber' Harris." He dropped the name to impress, but the young officers weren't. "However we do have the Special Boat Service."

"Never heard of it," Howling Mad snorted. "What's that when it's at home?"

Fleming sighed like a man sorely tried. He had been through this before with Commander Keith. Still, he kept his temper and started to explain: "The Special Boat Service is an off-shoot of the SAS." He looked pointedly at Howling Mad.

The latter nodded. He had heard of the SAS.

"Well for some time now they have been experimenting with what they call 'wave riders'." Before Howling Mad could query the term, Fleming said hastily, "Human torpedoes to you."

That impressed the young officers.

"And what have these SBS, er, 'wave riders' got to do with us?" Howling Mad asked.

"Commander I'm going to suggest that each of your motor-launches carries a two-man SBS team from now on. The two men on their chariot, as they call it, can direct a five-ton pack of high explosive at their target."

"But are they prepared to sacrifice their lives just like that, sir?" O'Rourke asked, impressed.

"Not exactly, O'Rourke, though they are chancing their arms obviously. No, what they do is to direct the chariot at their target and then when they are sure it's going to hit it they flop over the side and swim back to the mother ship, which in our case would be one of your motor-launches. This I think would be the only way to stop the *Tirpitz*."

Now, at last, they were impressed and Howling Mad

grunted, "Brave lot of buggers, your SBS. What are they, ex-marines?"

"Yes," Fleming answered.

"Thought so. They're all mad as March hares. Now when are they coming up from their base?"

"This very night, Commander," Fleming said. "The Admiralty and the London and North-Eastern Railway have given them top priority to bring themselves and their gear up to Hull."

"Good, then we'll do a bit of overtime – *unpaid*," Howling Mad said. "All hands will muster tonight to get them and their human torpedoes aboard as quickly as possible. I want to start patrolling at dawn tomorrow morning. I don't think we can afford to waste much time."

"I agree, Commander," Fleming said. "On Saturday Churchill comes to Hull. That gives us four short days. At the present time we think the *Tirpitz* is in Dutch waters. Our listening station at Scarborough picked up a signal, then the Wren operator who caught the damned thing had to go out and be sick before she could get the whole signal." He shrugged. "*Women*. Turns out she's pregnant by some brown job or other, an army man."

"How could she stoop so low?" one of the young officers chortled. "Fancy a Wren having sexual inter-course with a brown job! She should be dismissed from the Service!"

Howling Mad silenced him with a glance and growled, "Well, at the speeds the *Tirpitz* can make, if she's coming this way she'll have to slip anchor Thursday next at the latest. That gives us three days to start patrolling. It'll be nip-and-tuck, but if everyone puts his shoulder to the wheel we can make it. All right, no more hot air!" He looked pointedly at Fleming. "You young

165

officers prepare to brief your crews. Then we'll make arrangements to house these SBS wallahs and their gear." He looked around at their suddenly earnest faces and said, very quietly for him, "Remember, gentlemen, this is not some great game. This mission is possibly of vital importance to Britain and to the Empire. Winston Churchill must survive. Dismiss . . .!"

Hastily his officers rose to their feet, put on their caps, saluted and then hurried out into the thick white fog.

Not far away the man in the blue suit, sheltering in the cover of a dock gantry, watched them. The urgency of their pace told him all he wanted to know. They knew. He turned to the big deserter who had thrown the grenade. "Jack," he whispered. "They tumbled!"

"Ay," the deserter said in that slow, half-witted fashion of his, "the city's full of rozzers. 'Bout time to do a bunk!"

"That's what I've been thinking as well, Jack. Hull's gonna get too hot to hold us."

"What about the gash?" Jack asked as they stole away, dodging into a shed as another party of ratings marched by through the white fog, while ships' sirens sounded mournfully in the estuary.

The man in the blue suit considered for a moment, then he said, "It's worth a pony to me, Jack, to have shot of her."

"A pony, eh!" Jack echoed greedily. "That'd buy me a new identity card. Gimme a new start it would."

"I suppose it would, Jack," the man in the blue suit said, as the naval party passed and they came out on to the quay once more. He wished he could get rid of the deserter too, but he was too big and powerful for him to tackle. He presented a permanent danger, but he'd take a dive himself now. The deserter would be on his own then. He wouldn't be able to tell the authorities much once they caught up with him, which they would in the end.

"When?" the deserter asked as they headed for the tram stop on Hedon Road.

"Tonight. You'll find her at her usual hangout, the 'Cock and Bottle' pub."

The deserter laughed coarsely. "Proper name for her and her trade." He sniffed. "Won't get much more cock after tonight, though!"

The little man in the blue suit said nothing. Then the tram appeared from the fog and they were off.

Chapter Four

The wind came from the east. It was a bitter, relentless blast of ice-cold air straight from Siberia, turning everything white so that as the motor-launch crept through the pre-dawn darkness, the whole superstructure hung heavy with hoar-frost. And it was rising all the time, a wild virago, shrieking through the rigging, sweeping across the slick, treacherous decks.

O'Rourke, peering out from the bridge, was happy with it. The wind, he reasoned, would give them the cover they needed if there were enemy craft out there; and according to the reports that Commander Fleming had received just before the last briefing there were plenty of German vessels, surface and sub-surface, in the North Sea. "Remarkable Hun activity," he lectured the skippers who were taking out the first patrols of the day. "According to my sources, there hasn't been so much activity in our coastal waters since just after D-Day. So, gentlemen, let me say this to you, watch your backs!" Which was exactly what Lt. O'Rourke was doing at this very moment.

"What do you think, sir?" Harding asked as he, too, peered through the icy spray and spindrift lashing over the launch's deck. He had been present at Commander Fleming's briefing as well.

"I think the balloon's going to go up soon, Chiefie.

How and where, I don't know. But something's going to happen, I feel it in my bones."

All that the old chief petty officer felt in his bones was aches and pains, but he said, "Yes, I think you're right, sir. You know, when you've been in the Royal as long as I have, you get to sense when something's going to happen, and this morning I feel that it is."

"Now don't be going on about how long you've been in the Royal Navy," O'Rourke said with a laugh, "or the lads'll be teasing you about Nelson again, eh?"

"They wouldn't dare," the old sailor said.

O'Rourke changed the subject. "How are the SBS chaps settling down?" he asked.

"All right, sir. They've tucked themselves away nice and snug. Typical Marines. They allus know just how to get their frigging feet under the table."

"They seem nice chaps, Chiefie – and tough."

"Ay, I'll give you that," CPO Harding answered. "Wouldn't like to meet the pair on a dark night down some alley."

The reference escaped O'Rourke, but he guessed what the other man meant. The two SBS men, a young lieutenant and an older corporal, were quiet, but obviously very tough. Both had shoulders on them like oxen and even Bunts, who was inclined to have a loose mouth, had kept relatively silent, when he and the rest of the crew had met them.

Half hour later, O'Rourke stood both watches to. They were steaming about 20 miles off Spurn Point and he felt that if they were going to run into trouble, it would be about here. So it was wise to have every man available ready for action. Now the double lookouts were sweeping the sea with their glasses for the first sight of the enemy and the gun crews were at their posts. Even the two marines had volunteered to stand a watch, though O'Rourke felt there was no need for them at this moment. Yet every man counted, so now the young Marine officer stood next to O'Rourke scouring the grey, heaving waste of the sea for the first sight of an enemy, which all of them knew instinctively was there somewhere.

Time passed leadenly as the motor-launch rode through the sea at half-speed, for O'Rourke saw no reason to waste fuel until he was in contact with the enemy. The cook brought up cocoa. On the deck the lookouts and gunners were getting theirs laced with rum. It was against regulations, but O'Rourke knew the men needed it. It would keep their spirits up for a little while at least

"*Bearing green three – oh . . . sub!*" the lookout sang out abruptly.

O'Rourke felt that old thrill run through his body. The enemy had been spotted. He swung his glasses round. Beside him the Marine officer did the same. "Christ Almighty!" he exclaimed. "A Jerry sub!"

Harding grinned. What did the SBS man think it was, Yorkshire Pud and roast taties?

On the deck the gunner's mate was yelling out: "Range on one thousand . . . deflection zero!"

Now the whole ship tensed in anticipation of what was soon to come. As yet the German U-boat, lying barely glimpsed above the white-fringed waves, hadn't seen them. Soon, however, the fight would commence and all of the men on deck knew that the submarine had the advantage of them, if they didn't get it right at the beginning. Once the U-boat submerged they wouldn't stand much of a chance against those deadly torpedoes that the submarine carried.

"*Fire!*" the gunners' mate shouted.

On the foredeck the 6-pounder roared into life, shaking

the bridge and making it tremble. The Marine officer, watching the white-glowing shell hurtling towards the surprised ship yelled, "Whacko!!"

O'Rourke grinned despite the tension. He wished he could still be as naively enthusiastic for battle as that.

The shell slammed into the submarine and it reeled so much that the conning tower seemed to touch the water.

On the monkey island the machine-gunner fired burst after burst. O'Rourke could hear the empty cartridge cases clattering on the deck like metal rain. Suddenly all was noise and violent activity.

On the U-boat's deck men were falling, crumbling into shapeless heaps. Others ran back and forth along the littered deck, waving their arms and shouting like men demented. Others, their faces determined and bitter, fired back. One German sailor swung the Schmeisser machine-pistol he carried slung round his neck and loosed a vicious burst in the direction of the motor-launch. He knew he could not make the range, O'Rourke told himself, but it was his chance to hit back and he was going to take it.

Harmlessly the slugs ripped along the water 100 yards away and Sparks shouted, "Silly bugger! What did you think that—" He never finished, going down suddenly, staring, as if bewildered at the bright red blood arcing from his right arm. "Well I'll be fucked!" he exclaimed. "The bastard did it!"

Bullets were peppering the metal sides of the bridge like heavy tropical rain hitting a tin roof. Next to O'Rourke, the SBS officer cried, "Fuck this for a game of soldiers! They're trying to kill us!"

"It's customary in battle," O'Rourke shouted back over the hammering of the machine-guns and the thwack-wack of the 4-pounder.

"I know it is," the young Marine snorted back. "But it's bloody dangerous, isn't it?" He laughed.

Despite the danger, O'Rourke smiled. The SBS officer was a good sort. He was glad the Marine was on his side.

Then something totally unexpected happened. When the 4-pounder fired again there was a sudden great gleaming hole in the U-boat's hull, then a man started to clamber cautiously out of the conning tower and in his hand he held what looked like a white shirt. Very deliberately, as if he were taking great care that he would be seen, he started waving it back and forth.

A great howl of triumph went up from O'Rourke's crew.

"By Christ, sir!" Harding exclaimed. "The Jerry's surrendering!"

O'Rourke felt a tremendous sense of elation, but he tried to remain calm and professional. Of course, he'd get a gong for capturing a U-boat. Still he didn't want CPO Harding or the young SBS officer to see just how thrilled he was. "Wheel admidships," he ordered, keeping his voice deliberately low. "Stop engines. Stand by to board her." As the bells clanged, he stuck his head out of the bridge house door and called, "Keep your eyes peeled, gun crew! You never know, lads!"

"Ay, ay, sir," they said smartly, their red faces wreathed in smiles now. Just like they knew Mr O'Rourke would get a gong for this, they also knew they'd get a spot of extra leave. It wasn't every day that a Jerry submarine with its priceless code-books and Enigma coding machine was captured.

Slowly the boarding party under the command of the Marine officer and the burly corporal clambered on to the submarine's hull. On her wet, slippery deck, a dead gunner lay sprawled in a pool of his own blood. One by one they stepped over him and, with the SBS officer in the lead, revolver in hand, they advanced on the strangely silent conning tower, where the lone German kept waving the white shirt as if his life depended upon it. Then, as the Marine prepared to mount the tower, he dropped the garment with a sigh of relief and said, "*Kamerad*!"

"Okay," the SBS officer said, remembering that his father had always said when they had been in the trenches in the old war, "*Kamerad*", or "comrade", meant the Boche had surrendered. All the same he didn't lower his revolver.

He pushed by the man and glanced down into the interior of the submarine. A man lay sprawled out directly below, a white cap on his head. The young SBS officer knew that in U-boats only the skipper wore a white cap and this particular skipper was dying. Blood was pouring from a gaping ragged wound in his chest; and it was obvious that he had been shot at close range for he could see the black powder burns on the cloth around the wound.

The man with the white shirt saw the look on the Marine's face and he said, "We shoot . . . we shoot captain." He made a gesture with his thumb and forefinger as if he were pulling a trigger.

"Why?" the astonished Marine asked.

"Enough . . . enough war!"

A face appeared below next to the dying skipper. It was angry and bitter. "*Leutnant* Berger," the German snapped, the resentment in his harsh voice all too obvious. "The swine shot our captain because he wanted to go on. They said he should surrender. They said this was *Selbstmord*." Angrily he fumbled for the word in English, then said, "Suicide . . . a suicide command."

"Why?" the SBS officer asked again, totally confused by this strange situation.

"Because of the *Tirpitz*," the German officer answered bitterly. "They say we shall all die."

The SBS officer could hardly contain his excitement. They'd done it.

They'd picked up the outer screen of the Tirpitz!

Chapter Five

"*Doenitz!*"

Hartmann recognised the icy, determined voice at once.

"At your service, Grand Admiral," he snapped formally, automatically saluting. Doenitz was a good 150 kilometres away at the other end of the telephone line, but it was an instinctive reaction.

"You sail this night, Hartmann," Doenitz barked. "There's been trouble."

"Trouble?" Hartmann asked, his old doubts about this mission returning immediately.

"Yes, something which I never thought would ever happen again. It's damned 1918 all over again.* One of my U-boat crews has mutinied. From the last radio message the U-boat radio operator was able to send before the crew smashed the radio, the swine shot their captain and took over the ship."

"I see, sir," Hartmann said, though he didn't really.

"It is pretty clear," Doenitz continued in that harsh, clipped fashion of his, "that the crew didn't want to go ahead with this vital mission of ours. If I had my way, I would shoot every man-jack of them out of hand,

* In 1918 part of the German Navy mutinied and threw their officers overboard. It was the beginning of the revolution against the German monarchy.

175

without trial. But I'm not in that position. However, what is important to you is that when the Tommies start to quiz and interrogate the mutineers they'll sing like canaries, the treacherous pigdogs!"

"Yes, I suppose, sir," Hartmann answered, his face worried now. Outside his cabin a sailor with a typical Hamburg waterfront accent was singing the popular song of the year, "*After every December there'll be another May ... Everything goes by ... everything will pass.*" Hartmann wondered whether the unknown sailor would be right but he didn't think so somehow. Then he concentrated once again on Doenitz. "But if they sing, *Herr Grossadmiral*, as you think they will, won't our mission be hopelessly compromised right from the start?"

"Naturally," Doenitz agreed swiftly. "But I doubt if they'll be able to stop you at night on the voyage out."

"And on returning, sir?" Hartmann said, his voice hard and intent.

Doenitz didn't answer the question. Instead, he said, "We all have to take great risks, Hartmann. It's the nature of our profession."

"But I have over a thousand young men aboard, young men who will be Germany's future."

"Hartmann, there will be *no* future for Germany if we lose this war," Doenitz barked categorically. "Don't you realise that? We know the Anglo-Americans' plans and those of the Russians. Our heavy industry will be destroyed and for our Fatherland the clock will be turned back to the Middle Ages. We shall become a peasant and agricultural economy once more. So my dear fellow, up anchor tonight and do your duty." Suddenly there was a note of what seemed envy in the Grand Admiral's harsh bitter voice, "God, how I wish I could sail with you,

Hartmann, and die a fighting sailor's death – a clean naval death and have done with it!" Doenitz pulled himself together swiftly. "But that is not to be. Good luck, Hartmann. Heil Hitler!"

"Heil Hitler!" Hartmann echoed without enthusiasm. The phone went dead.

Outside, the man with the waterfront accent had stopped singing. Perhaps, he, too, knew now that there was going to be no new May for him.

Hartmann thought for a moment or two. First he considered his own position. Naturally he couldn't survive an operation of this kind, because when the Allies won the war, they would shoot him – and he knew the Russians and the Anglo-Americans would win. There was no doubt of that.

Naturally, for Hartmann had always been taught that his men's safety came before his, he didn't dwell on what might happen to him. He thought of the young men under his command. They wouldn't survive, he knew that already. So what was he supposed to do? Could he do what this unknown U-boat crew – the 'pigdogs', as Doenitz had castigated them – had done, surrender without a fight?

In the silence of his cabin, he shook his head and, talking to himself in the fashion of lonely men, he said, "No, that would be quite out of the question. I could never surrender. It is a question of honour."

He pulled a face, wishing suddenly that he had never volunteered for the Navy as an enthusiastic 18-year-old straight from the *Gymnasium*, where in 1923 his teachers had told him, "There's no future in the Navy, young Hartmann. You're wasting your life! Germany will never be an important military power again. The Allies won't allow it. Pah! Military service is a sheer waste of time and intellect!"

"All the same you did volunteer," he told himself. "So what are you going to do now?" Even as he posed the question *Kapitan zur See* Hartmann knew the answer.

"*Duty!*" he announced firmly, as if he were addressing the ship's company. "Hartmann, you will do your duty as you always have done." Face set and determined, he picked up the desk telephone. "Dietz!" he snapped, when his Number One answered. "Please come to my cabin immediately. We have work to do!"

Fleming looked at Howling Mad and his officers. "We've got 'em!" he announced triumphantly.

"You think so?" Howling Mad replied. "There's many a slip between cup and lip, remember, Fleming."

The Naval Intelligence officer ignored the comment. He was too full of himself to be deflected now. "Yes, young O'Rourke says that the U-boat Huns are babbling all over the place. The *Tirpitz* is in the Dutch naval port of Den Heldern." He walked swiftly over to the big map of the North Sea on the wall of Howling Mad's office and pointed to the port on the northern coast of Occupied Holland. "There she is. Obviously she'll stick to the Dutch coast as long as she can, where she's protected by her own aircraft. Then somewhere, perhaps here, about the Rotterdam area, she'll commence her dash across the North Sea."

Howling Mad made a quick calculation. "At the speed the *Tirpitz* can move," he said after a moment, "she'll arrive off our coast in about 12 hours. And at this time of the year it's dark for all that time. So she'll be a difficult target to locate, visually at least."

178

"Exactly, Commander," Fleming agreed. "My thinking exactly."

"What is being done then?" Keith asked.

"Well, Met says the weather's going to be lousy for the next 2 hours. The usual for this time of the year – fog, rain, sleet and snow. That'll make contact difficult and it rules out air support I suppose. I heard from the Admiralty just before this briefing that they are sending two cruisers down from Scapa and a handful of destroyers, but I doubt if the cruisers will make it in time."

"Damned tincans! No earthly use at the best of times!" Howling Mad snorted and his young officers smirked. They all knew his antipathy towards large ships. As he was wont to proclaim, "The day of the battleship is over. These days it's up to us in the little craft to bring home the bacon!"

"So, gentlemen," Fleming said with an air of finality, "it's going to be up to you, it seems, and our comrades of the SBS." He looked at Howling Mad. "What's the drill now, Commander?"

"As soon as O'Rourke enters the mouth of the Humber and can fill us with further details of whatever information he has got from the Hun U-boat, we'll see a prize crew is put on board her and then the whole flotilla will go on patrol."

There was a murmur of excitement from the young officers.

"Every craft will take a grid section to patrol, but keeping in touch with each other. As soon as we spot the *Tirpitz* we will be after her like a shot. We won't let her get away."

"Here, here!" someone said and Howling Mad flashed the speaker a hard, fierce look.

"It's not going to be easy," he continued. "Not damn easy at all. You can take my word for that."

"I take your point, Commander," Fleming agreed. "But I pray you and your fellows will succeed. If you don't there might well be national tragedy."

"How do you mean, Fleming?"

"Over the last few hours I have been doing some thinking about *Tirpitz* and what her mission is. Why is the Hun prepared to lose the greatest battleship in the world? What mission could be so important?"

"Well, Commander, what conclusion have you come up with?" Howling Mad asked impatiently, his mind already busy with the details of the action to come.

"As we know now, 30-odd years ago the German High Seas Fleet cocked a snoot at the Royal Navy by bombarding the coast of Yorkshire."

"Yes, yes. We've already been through that, Fleming!"

"That action was nothing much more than an act of defiance, showing the greatest fleet in the world at that time that the German Navy was something to be reckoned with. This time it's going to be totally different."

"How?"

"If the *Tirpitz* gets into the Humber—"

"What?" Howling Mad interrupted, aghast. "What did you just say, Fleming?"

"If the *Tirpitz* gets into the Humber, the target for her guns and any commandos she might have on board will be Mr Churchill. I'm totally convinced of that."

For a few moments even Howling Mad was at a loss for words, he was so shocked. Finally he faltered, "You really think so?"

"I do! It's taken me a long time to put all the bits and pieces of this mosaic together, but that's what it is." Fleming looked grimly at Howling Mad, his usual languid manner absent. "Under the present circumstances, you and your chaps are the only people standing in the path of the Hun ship. If you don't stop the *Tirpitz*—" he shrugged and left the rest of his sentence unfinished.

Howling Mad shook his head violently like a man trying to wake out of some nightmarish dream. "We'll do our best, Fleming, you can rely on that." With surprisingly formality he held out his right hand and Fleming took the hard horny palm in his own and pressed it hard.

At the other side of the North Sea, 300 miles away, Captain Hartmann did the same to Dietz, saying, "Well, Number One, the die is cast. There's no turning back now."

Dietz nodded and the great ship started to slip into the night, a predator out looking for its prey.

Chapter Six

Captain Hartmann touched his hand to his cap in return to the salute of the young officer on the bridge. The *Tirpitz* was sliding smoothly through the night, perhaps ten sea miles off the Dutch coast. There was no moon and Dietz had posted double lookouts. Down below, the radar crews were working flat out. But their screens remained free of any sightings.

"Good-evening, Lahn," Hartmann said in that pleasant fashion of his which endeared him to his crew. "Anything out of the ordinary to report?"

"No sir," the handsome young officer replied, using the standard formula, "No special circumstances to report, sir."

Hartmann smiled. Some of these wartime officers were more formal than the regulars with years of service behind them. "What did you do before the war, Lahn?" he asked idly, as his experienced eye flashed round the bridgehouse checking that everyone was doing his job properly.

"I was a student of theology at Heidelberg, sir," Lahn replied, slightly embarrassed by the admission.

"Theology, eh." Hartmann rolled the word over his tongue, as if it were important. "Were you going to be a pastor?"

"Yes sir."

"A good profession! When I was just younger than

you, I wasn't studying theology, I was the scum of the earth, a sailing cadet on what was called a school-ship. Hell with sails, we called it." He chuckled at the memory, while the young officer looked at him slightly puzzled, wondering probably why the skipper was telling him all this. "We scrubbed the decks, never got much more than a couple of hours sleep a night, and lived off swill that no normal farmer would ever feed to his pigs. Naturally, I could have gone to university, too. I had the *Abitur*," – the German high-school leaving certificate. "But I wanted the hell with sails. I wanted to become a regular naval officer because I knew this war would happen one day. I would command a great ship like *Tirpitz*."

"Yes sir, I understand, sir," Lahn said hastily, although he didn't.

Hartmann forgot the past. He concentrated on the present now, knowing that he held Lahn's fate and that of all the other young men in his hand. It was an awesome responsibility. "Keep a weather eye open, Lahn," he ordered. "Sooner or later the Tommies will pick us up on their radar. As soon as the radar men below report that they have a contact, please let me know at once."

"*Zu Befehl, Herr Kapitan*," Lahn answered promptly and clicked to attention once more.

Hartmann nodded and left the bridge. Then he commenced his usual inspection of the ship. He always liked night inspections. A ship then was surprisingly quiet, the only real sound the efficient throb of the turbines. In fact, it seemed almost as if the crew had deserted the *Tirpitz*. Here and there there was a lookout, of course. But otherwise the 1000-odd men who manned the great ship had apparently vanished.

He walked towards the bows and paused underneath

the great forward turret. These guns would do the job, he supposed. He stared up at the two long 15in barrels capable of shooting accurately over 20 kilometres. What havoc they would wreak soon, he told himself. Suddenly he felt an icy finger of fear trace its way down his spine. He shivered and said to himself, "Hartmann, a louse just ran over your liver."

Suddenly he smiled, perhaps at himself, he didn't know. Hartmann, old friend, he thought, you'll just have to accept your fate, and with that he turned and started to make his way aft to his cabin. There was nothing more he could do, but carry out his orders to the bitter end.

"Sir." Howling Mad turned.

It was the radio operator. His young face was flushed with excitement as he held the message form ready to hand it to the skipper.

"What is it?"

"Scarborough has picked her up, the *Tirpitz*, sir!" the excited young rating blurted out. "Here you are – the bearing, everything!"

Howling Mad grabbed the paper and read the signal. His assessment of the previous day had been corrected. The *Tirpitz* had just left the Dutch coast some 12 sea miles off Rotterdam and was heading straight into the area being patrolled by his flotilla. In fact they would be entering that section of the sea where he had already decided he would concentrate his flotilla once the *Tirpitz* had been spotted.

He handed the radio operator the message for filing and ordered: "Signal all the skippers. Pass on the bearing. Tell them to concentrate."

"Ay ay, sir." The operator sped away as Howling Mad turned to the young fair-headed SBS officer who had been listening eagerly to the conversation. "I think it's about time to get yourself ready and arm your – er – wave rider. Don't envy you your task, but we'll do our best to pick you up afterwards."

"I'm sure you will, sir," the young Marine officer replied gratefully as they shook hands. "Well, I'd better be off and alert my corporal."

Now, as the flotilla of little boats began to concentrate, racing through the night at top speed to get into position, all was hectic activity. The chariots were armed. The SBS men changed into their frogman suits. Winches and gantries were set ready to launch them over the sides of the speeding boats. Gunners took up their positions and double lookouts were posted; the radio operators tensed over their sets, waiting for further signals on the *Tirpitz*'s position.

The hours passed. Working over his charts and trying to guess at what speed the *Tirpitz*'s captain might be moving at night in wartime when ships sailed without riding lights, though the great battleship would have radar of course, Howling Mad guessed they would meet the enemy just after three that morning. Naturally, in order to get the chariots within a suitable range, they'd be close enough for the *Tirpitz*'s radar to pick them up on the screens and identify them as British. But with their speed and small size they might be able to evade the enemy gunners. It was a question of launching the chariots and then racing away until the SBS caught up with them. Howling Mad straightened up from the little chart-table and frowned. Somehow he knew the SBS men wouldn't make it, but as long as they slammed their chariots into the side of the enemy battleship their sacrifice would not have been in vain.

By now the signals from Scarborough were coming in more frequently. There were other signals, too, coming directly from the Admiralty informing him of the radio messages which the *Tirpitz's* captain was transmitting back to his own HQ. Howling Mad rightly supposed that Naval Intelligence had cracked the code of the German navy, the *Kriegsmarine*.

Then came the signal Howling Mad had been waiting for in anticipation, but also with some apprehension, for the last hour or so. It was from O'Rourke, simple and direct: '*T. sighted.*'

O'Rourke had spotted the *Tirpitz*!

"Object on port bow!" the shout broke into O'Rourke's reverie as he stood on the swaying deck of the motor-launch, drinking a mug of scalding hot cocoa and savouring the warm steam rising about his face.

O'Rourke acted immediately. The cocoa went over the side and the tin mug fell to the deck with a clatter. "Where?" he demanded, reaching for his powerful night glasses.

"Green-one-zero, sir," the lookout answered smartly.

O'Rourke turned in the direction indicated and gasped when that long, lean, dangerous shape slid into his lenses. It seemed to go on for ever – a monster of a ship, a stark, sinister black outline, bare of lights and at that distance giving off no sound. It could well have been the *Marie Celeste*, that mysterious, abandoned vessel, found with no one aboard.

But O'Rourke, his mind racing, knew that the battle-ship was crewed all right. By young determined men, who would snuff out their lives if given the chance.

The young SBS officer came running up. "Heard the lookout," he panted. "Is it the *Tirpitz*?"

O'Rourke couldn't see the details of his features too well in the darkness, but he could sense the Marine's excitement and tension. "Yes, it's the *Tirpitz* all right," he said quietly, trying to keep his own excitement under control.

"Do we attack?"

O'Rourke shook his head. "Not yet. Got to signal Howl – er Commander Keith and wait for orders."

Now the radioman came doubling up with Howling Mad's order: 'Shadow her, but don't risk your ship,' then the first star shells began to explode over the heaving green sea, turning night into day. The *Tirpitz*'s radar had picked them up.

"Dammit it, Dietz!" Hartmann cursed. "It's too early! I wanted to be off the English coast before they spot-ted us!"

Dietz shrugged. "Sorry, sir. But they have."

"Yes, of course," Hartmann said, calming himself immediately. He had long realised that a commanding officer must never show his inner feelings and tensions to his subordinates. It unsettled them. "Have you identified the Tommy?" he asked, as yet another star shell exploded from the flare gun aft.

"Not yet, sir. The ship's dancing all over the radar screen."

"That means it's a very small craft," Hartmann concluded immediately. "Not one that could present any danger to us – *at the moment*. Naturally the Tommy will be already signalling his home base that we're here."

"Of course, sir," Dietz agreed. "He's out there shadowing us. But sir," he smiled confidently, "what can she to do us? Or what else is left of the Royal Navy in their home waters? As for those air gangsters of theirs who have ruined our cities, they won't be able to fly in the weather predicted for the next few days. All in all, sir, I think we can say we are relatively safe."

Hartmann smiled a little. "I am glad you are so confident! I hope the men are too." His smile vanished. "But you can never tell with the Tommies. The English are a cunning, devious people. They might have something up their sleeves we don't know about."

"I should think, sir, that by the time they pull anything from their sleeves we shall have completed our mission and then it will be too late."

"I hope you're right, Dietz," Hartmann answered. Outside, another star shell exploded.

"All right," Howling Mad snapped to his radio operator. "Lieutenant O'Rourke has been spotted, as we will be in due course. I want you to signal this to all skippers: '*Attack from port and starboard. Co-ordinate attacks with each other. No mix-ups. Main thing, keep the Hun gunners guessing*'." Suddenly he gave the signaller a wintry smile, a rare gesture from him. "And add '*England expects*'. They'll know what I mean!"

"Yes sir." The rating turned smartly, telling himself that the old man had got a bit of the old Nelsonitis.

As for Howling Mad, he sat there for a moment, ruminating. He was not an imaginative man but he

188

guessed this present attack was going to be the epitome of his career. He'd never do anything more important or better. Ever since he had been a 14-year-old cadet at Dartmouth he had somehow known his naval career would end like this: death in some last desperate action.

Surprisingly enough the thought didn't worry him one bit.

Chapter Seven

Churchill beamed at the wine waiter as the train thundered through the night from King's Cross. "Ah!" he said jovially, "it's almost peacetime again, I see. A wine waiter!"

Sitting opposite him General Ismay, Churchill's military adviser, shook his head in mock wonder. The PM didn't realise that this had been specially laid on for him. The troops travelling north on this same route, would usually take 11 to 12 hours, whereas this one would rival the record set up by the 'Flying Scotsman' in 1936 of two and half hours. They would be lucky if they got a cup of milkless and sugarless tea. Indeed they would be lucky even to get a cup. The good ladies of the WVS, who manned the station canteens, usually served the foul liquid in old jam jars. But Ismay said nothing as Churchill ordered his usual brandy plus a bottle of pre-war Chateau Rothschild, with, "I hope it has not been shaken too badly."

The wine waiter said gravely, "The L.N.E.R takes the greatest care with its wines, sir." Outside he said under his breath in the accent of his native Glasgow, "Shaken too frigging badly! Wait till yon Major Attlee of Labour gets in, then the frigging heads'll roll!"

Churchill stared at the menu, again with foods especially prepared for him, though he did not know

190

this. He took little interest in food as long as it was there and good. Food, like so many things in his life, was a matter for domestics. Colville, his secretary, said, "That chap from Naval Intelligence, Fleming, sir. You remember him?"

Churchill nodded absently.

"Well, he called and informed me that the *Tirpitz* has sailed. Again he asked me to warn you about Hull tomorrow."

Churchill looked up. "Fellah was a journalist before the war. *The Times*—"

"*Sunday Times*," Colville corrected him.

"Well, you know what these journalist johnnies are like. They always like to sensationalise things, don't they!"

General Ismay, a short dark man with a Jewish cast of features, laughed. "Well, you should know better than we do, PM. You were a journalist yourself for long enough!"

"Only for the money, the filthy lucre was sorely needed in those pre-war days." He grew more serious. "What are their Lordships doing about the *Tirpitz*?" he asked.

"They've thrown a flotilla of motor torpedo launches in the path of the Hun," Colville answered, "so Commander Fleming tells me. Each launch carries a Special Boat Service team, who will attack the *Tirpitz* with chariots." He looked inquiringly at the Prime Minister. "You've heard of the device, sir?"

"Of course I have!" Churchill snorted, looking over the top of his half-moon spectacles at his young secretary indignantly. "I'll have you know I suggested the device to the Admiralty after the Italians had used something similar against our warships off Gibraltar." He sniffed. "Is that all?"

"Yes, at present, sir."

Churchill considered. Almost as if to himself, he muttered, "Brave young men . . . brave young men, all of them. I wonder how many of them will come back . . .?"

A hundred miles farther north, a wide-awake Fleming worried. Outside even at this hour, there was still hammering going on as the labourers worked into the night to get the stands ready for the great Home Guard standing down parade. For hours now Fleming had been dividing his time between signalling to Commander Keith and attempts to get the various local authorities to provide better protection for the Prime Minister. But he had achieved little. The air raid services were going on a full 24-hour alert. The local coastal fighter stations were also standing by for immediate action, but all the heavy bomber stations at Sutton, Linton and Holmfirth farther inland had been grounded. The weather was too bad. He had even talked with a crusty brigadier in charge of the Hull area Home Guard, who would lead the parade, and asked him if he couldn't think of some pretext to cancel the whole business.

The old soldier, with his sweeping moustache, which probably dated back to the Boer War, and a purple face due probably to years of indulgence in good port, had exploded, "Good gad, sir! Can't do that! My chaps have been looking forward to this for weeks. Can't disappoint the chaps, y'know. Besides after five years of it, working all hours, they deserve this parade. The Lord Mayor's throwing them a shindig afterwards, too. You know, tea and buns, and ham sandwiches." He had pronounced the words with great emphasis as if ham sandwiches were a very important treat. "No sir. A cancellation is totally out of the question!"

Now he slumped there, worried, in his battered leather armchair with the stuffing coming out. He had done the job he had come up to Hull to do – he had solved the mystery. At the same time if anything did happen to the Prime Minister, he would be the one who would have to take the can back. Their Lordships of the Admiralty would need a scapegoat for the tragedy. He could see the headlines already: 'NAVAL COMMANDER HELD RESPONSIBLE FOR DEATH OF PRIME MINISTER'. And that would be the end of his plans for a brilliant post-war career as a writer. His name would be mud in the publishing world, he knew that.

In the end he gave up. He put on his tunic and greatcoat and went out into the freezing darkness. Ten minutes later he was at Howling Mad's little headquarters. The shore staff, looking unshaven and harassed, were working flat out. Teleprinters clattered, telephones rang urgently. Young sailors hurried back and forth with papers in their hands. All was bustling, hectic activity.

He entered the office of the young flag officer, who was in charge in Howling Mad's absence, and said, "Well?"

The young officer looked up, startled. His face was very pale and there were dark circles under his eyes. "Oh, Commander Fleming! Well, sir, we've just received a signal from the flotilla commander."

"And?" Fleming demanded urgently.

"Commander Keith's going to lead the first strike himself, sir."

Under his breath, Fleming prayed fervently for the

first time since he had left Eton. Aloud he said, "Let's hope for God's sake he makes it, Lieutenant."

Numbly the other officer nodded his agreement.

Hartmann was on deck again. The small English craft which had been shadowing them had vanished into the pre-dawn gloom. But he knew the others were still out there. There were at least nine dots on the radar screens indicating that there was a flotilla of them, though he couldn't imagine what they intended doing against the might of the *Tirpitz*.

He stared moodily to his front, remembering the time he had been second officer on the *Graf Spee* back in 1939. His skipper, Hans Langsdorff, had been intensely proud of his pocket battleship, as it was popularly called, and his record. In two months he had destroyed nine British ships, totalling 50,000 tons, without losing a single man. Time and time again he had evaded British ships, his name making the headlines all around the globe. In that December of 1939 Langsdorff had been on top of the world, feeling that nothing in the South Atlantic could stop him or his beloved *Graf Spee*. Yet within a matter of days his whole proud reputation had been shattered by the Tommies' superior tactics. He had seen no other way out but to scuttle the *Graf Spee* and shoot himself in the head out of shame.

"*Wie gekommen so zerronnen*, Easy come, easy go," Hartmann whispered to himself, staring at the white-flecked dark sea, thinking of those far off days and realising yet again as he had many times during the long war that nothing was certain but the unexpected.

He sniffed and wished he could light one of his 'evil weeds,' as he called the black cigars he favoured, but he knew he couldn't. At night, no one was allowed to smoke on deck, not even the skipper. He pulled up the collar of his greatcoat, the pre-dawn cold was bone-chilling. He listened to the satisfying, pulsating throb of the *Tirpitz's* engines. It wouldn't be long now, he told himself. For better or worse they would soon commence their mission.

Suddenly he started. The klaxons were shrilling 'Action stations' once again. Gunners in flash gear started running on to the deck to their weapons. This was it!

Captain Hartmann narrowed his eyes and stared to port, as the first star shells began to explode in bursts of blinding, incandescent light. There was something out there. He could just see, coming at them fast, very fast. It was the enemy all right, he knew that instinctively, and this time they were coming in to the attack.

Hurriedly he sprinted to the bridge and flung open the door of the bridgehouse. In that very same instant the Oerlikons began to blast, their four barrels between them pumping over 1000 20mm shells a minute at the bold intruder.

Suddenly, surprisingly, the racing motor-launch made a great bold curve, turning broadsides on to that lethal white wall of shells. Hartmann stared, puzzled, at the spectacle. Had the Tommy skipper gone mad, exposing his little craft like that? Then the motor-launch was racing away, followed by glowing, angry tracer shells, but behind it it left something else moving low in the water towards the battleship.

"What in three devils' names—" he began. Then he realised what it was. "*Kampf-schwimmer!*" he cried in sudden alarm. "Battle swimmer. Get the port gunners on to the damn thing before it's too late!"

The chariot, barely visible above the surface of the sea, hurried towards the monstrous bulk of the great ship: its five tons of high explosive would certainly stop the *Tirpitz* if the battleship was hit. The gunners knew it. Their lives depended on stopping the almost invisible little craft before it was too late. Frantically, dripping sweat despite the biting cold, the machine-gunners blasted away at the vehicle of death. Red and white tracer criss-crossed the intervening space. It seemed no one could survive such a volume of deadly fire, but still the chariot came on.

"Star shells!" Hartmann yelled like a man demented. "Illuminate the whole shitting area – *QUICK*!" Now he was too worried about the fate of his ship to control his emotions and fears.

The first . . . second . . . third flare hissed into the night sky. Plop! Abruptly, night was turned into day. The whole area was lit by the unearthly glowing light.

The chariot was now only half a kilometre away. But in that harsh brilliance it could no longer hide itself. The gunners started to aim more carefully. Then it happened. There was a tremendous flash of angry red flame followed by a huge boom. For a few moments the sea hissed and boiled like a live creature. Then as the firing started to falter, there was silence. The first attack on the *Tirpitz* had failed.

Chapter Eight

Some joked. "After you Cecil. No, after you Claud!" they cracked after the characters in Tommy Handley's 'ITMA', the popular radio show. "Going down, sir ... Don't forget the diver!" Others were sombre and businesslike, checking the frogman's gear and masks, patting each other as they prepared to launch the chariots, ensuring that all their gear was in place. Others remained very British and stiff-upper-lipped, with, "Good egg! I think we'll see off the Hun this time!"

Yet all of them had seen the crazy firing on the horizon, followed by that tremendous explosion which indicated that one of the chariots had exploded before it had reached its target.

On his motor-launch, O'Rourke patted the shoulder of the young SBS lieutenant, the only way he could express his feelings to a man dressed in a rubber suit and said, "Good luck, old chap!"

"Oh, I think all will be well on the night," the Marine quipped. "We'll pull it off – as the actress said to the bishop, what!"

O'Rourke forced himself to laugh. He didn't tell the Marine that he had just received a signal from Howling Mad that the first attack had failed disastrously. "Well, we'll get your craft within the prescribed distance, pause, drop you from the gantry and then pull off out of the

197

range of their machine-guns at least. That's the drill anyway," he added not very confidently.

"Sounds all right to me," the Marine answered easily, as if preparing for some jaunt and not a possible suicide mission.

"The Commander," O'Rourke meant Keith, "thought he might be able to do the job without risking the rest of the flotilla. Unfortunately it didn't work out like that. So it's going to be a mass attack this time."

"Good tactic," the Marine answered in the same manner as before, busily engaged in arranging his rubber cuffs so that his frogman's suit would remain perfectly watertight. "I think it's about time we got into our seats. Corporal."

"Sir." The husky-looking NCO followed the officer towards the chariot in that strange waddle they had to adopt to walk on dry land.

O'Rourke turned and hurried back to the bridge where Harding shook his head a little sadly and said, "Brave young lads, sir, brave young lads!" For a moment O'Rourke thought he caught the glimpse of tears in Harding's eyes, then the old CPO said, "The Commander has just signalled that Mr Reece will carry his chariot in first. He'll be coming in on our port side so we'll have to watch out—" He didn't finish the sentence, for suddenly the two of them saw Reece's boat skimming across the dark water to their right, heading straight for the giant battleship.

Immediately the German gunners opened fire. Again tracer, red, white and green criss-crossed the sea in a terrible cross fire. A moment later the 20mm Oerlikons started pumping away. It seemed that no one could get through that wall of deadly fire. But Reece's boat appeared to bear a charmed life. Time and time again when O'Rourke, his fingernails pressed into his palms with tension until his hands hurt, thought Reece had not survived, the racing launch came through yet again.

Suddenly the launch slowed. The man at the winch let the chariot drop into the water in the same instant that Reece swung his craft. The watchers could see the splash as the huge chunk of mobile high explosive hit the water. Next instant the chariot was hurrying towards its target as Reece swung his craft round and prepared to race for the rear. But now the young officer's luck had finally run out. Suddenly the launch seemed to leap out of the water as a giant blowtorch of vicious flame seared the length of the stricken craft's deck. The two watchers on the bridge caught a glimpse of tiny figures wreathed in flame flinging themselves overboard or writhing on the burning deck, their struggles getting weaker by the instant. Slowly the burning launch started to sink by the bow.

"Poor sods!" Harding said softly and crossed himself.

O'Rourke shook his head in despair. "Let's hope their sacrifice has been worth while," he whispered, as if to himself.

The two hooded charioteers were firmly astride their deadly weapon, heading straight for the monstrous ship which seemed to fill the whole horizon. At a steady three and a half knots, barely visible above the waves, they were steering for *Tirpitz's* midships, steering the chariot by means of a primitive rudder.

Both the SBS men were volunteers and were champion swimmers, hardened by swimming naked in the coldest of waters in winter, but they knew they stood little chance of being picked up now. Still, they persisted in their suicide mission, as if unaware that in a few minutes they might both be dead 50 miles or more from the coast of England.

Now the *Tirpitz* loomed up, ever larger. There seemed no end to her. Men were running along her deck carrying rifles and stick-grenades. The two SBS men knew why. Now the fire from the machine-guns high above on her deck was passing harmlessly above their heads. The throb-throb of the battleship grew louder and louder. It was time to dive. The Number One, who steered the chariot, raised his thumb, it was time to dive. Number Two, who sat astern, nodded his understanding. Up above on the battleship's deck sailors were lying flat on their stomachs, firing low. Others were tossing stick-grenades over the sides. Time and time again the water erupted in wild white fury.

Number One flooded the main ballast tank. Then he pumped water into the two trimming tanks, and the two brave young Marines were submerged save for their heads.

Gently Number One eased the joystick forward. The nose of the chariot commenced a light, downward slope. Both men seemed oblivious to the threshing and heaving of the water caused by the small-arms fire and grenades. Down they went deeper and deeper. The pale green water became ever darker. Number One kept his eye glued to the green-glowing needle of the depth gauge showing, *10ft . . . 15ft . . . 20ft . . .* Deep enough. Carefully he pulled back on the joystick. The chariot flattened out perfectly.

Even at their present depth, the two of them could hear the powerful throb of engines as the *Tirpitz*'s hull came into view. A red-grey shape moving through the water directly ahead. They had only a minute or so before they would be churned to bloody pulp by the battleship's great screws. Number One's ears were filled with a terrible buzzing pain, his nose was beginning to bleed under the water pressure.

Number One turned the chariot so that it was now running parallel with the *Tirpitz*'s hull. Not a second could be lost, the Number One knew, for at the speed the *Tirpitz* was making she would soon lose them. Both men reached out their right hands in unison. There was a hollow boom at the first magnets were attached. The chariot was now being carried along at a tremendous rate by their victim. It was a thought that gave the Number One a great deal of pleasure despite the terrible pain he was in.

Then two more magnets were hastily attached to the battleship's hull.

Holding on grimly with his right hand to the magnet, the Number Two went to work to release the high-explosive container. There was a hollow boom as he finally released it. Now it was firmly attached to the *Tirpitz*'s hull.

He released his throbbing right arm, red-hot pain surging down its length. Hurriedly he tapped his partner on the shoulder; they had five minutes to clear the enemy ship.

Number One set 'Slow ahead' and adjusted the plates to 'Hard to rise' and the chariot rose steeply. A moment later they had broken surface, tossing and bobbing in the great battleship's mighty wake like a cork in a maelstrom.

The two Marines swallowed and swallowed, fighting against the air pressure which threatened to burst their eardrums at any moment. It was at that moment that tragedy struck. Unknown to them, a German Marine had been waiting for them to re-surface. Boldly he had climbed down the side of the hull of the *Tirpitz* and, balancing himself as best he could, he was positioned there, waiting for them to come into his sights. Then he saw them. He didn't hesitate. The machine-pistol slung around his shoulder by a leather strap chattered. Number One screamed briefly as his chest was torn apart by the first burst. He flung up his arms like a man in absolute despair, then he disappeared over the side. The Number Two's face was shot to ribbons by the next burst. It looked like a ball of molten red wax, flecked here and there by the glistening white of splintered bone. He slumped in the bottom of the craft, carried away into eternity.

Howling Mad raged. "Two launches gone!" He bayed. "For nothing . . . for frigging damned nothing! God Almighty! I could pull my bloody hair out if I had any!"

At any other time his Number One would have laughed. Not now. For although it seemed clear that the chariot had succeeded in getting underneath the *Tirpitz*, the great ship was intact. There had been no explosion and the enemy battleship was still steaming towards England at full speed. "Perhaps they failed to connect the charge. Perhaps something was defective—"

"Damn-well doesn't matter one farthing!" Howling Mad interrupted him harshly. "She's still intact." His face bitter, he made up his own mind. "Number One we've got to stop the Hun bastard before it's too late, cost what it may. Signal all skippers. *'Maximum effort. Tirpitz must be sunk. Spare no cost!'*"

The younger officer looked at him aghast. "Do you mean—" he began to stutter.

"I do," Howling Mad cut him short once again. "Even if they have to sacrifice their own lives to do so. Winnie's more important than any of us. Send that signal. We either sink the *Tirpitz* or we don't come home, and that includes you and me . . ."

On the bridge of *Tirpitz*, Hartmann breathed a sigh of relief after the Chief Engineer had made his report. "So you think, Lutz, that the limpet mine or whatever they've stuck to our hull is defective?"

"*Jawohl, Herr Kapitan*," the young officer reported promptly. He indicated the doctor's stethoscope hanging from his neck. "I crawled into the bulkhead compartment till I found the place where the Tommies attached the thing and listened hard." He puffed out his lips, perhaps with contempt. "Not a sound. Another example of defective English engineering. They don't know how to produce effective weapons the way we Germans do."

Hartmann ignored the comment. Instead he said, "Well that's a damned weight off my mind. For a moment I thought the tick-tock was really in the pisspot, as we used to say in the old days. Still, next time we might not be so lucky." He rose and went over to the bridge telephone. "Guns," he ordered smartly. "Tell Guns to report to the bridge immediately. It's very urgent."

Quickly, 'Guns', the chief gunner, reported to the bridge. He was a big serious-looking man, older than most of the other ship's officers – and clever. Most gunnery officers were. "Sir," he reported.

Hartmann wasted no time. "You know the position, Guns," he snapped. "There are still about six or seven of the Tommies out there. They are dancing all over the radar screen, trying to keep out of the range of quick-firers and small arms."

Guns nodded his understanding.

"Well, they'll attack again, I'm damned sure of that.

Next time they might be lucky with those fiendish devices of theirs. So I want them knocked out before they can get within range. I want you to turn the big boys on them."

Guns whistled. "That'd be like trying to swat a fly with a sledge-hammer, sir!"

"I know, I know," Hartmann answered impatiently. "But it's got to be done. We've done so much and come so far. I don't want to lose my lovely *Tirpitz* to some shitting Tommy bumboat."

"*Zu Befehl, Herr Kapitan,*" the chief gunnery officer touched his hand to the peak of his cap. Then he was gone.

Five minutes later, the address system broke into metallic life. "Now hear this," the chief mate snapped. "Here this . . . clear the decks . . . clear the decks, the 15in turrets are going into action!"

Chapter Nine

The *Tirpitz*'s great guns opened fire. Eight huge cannon blasting away at the tiny launches racing towards the battleship. The grey dawn sky was torn apart. Even those sheltering below decks held their hands to their ears, mouths open so that their eardrums wouldn't burst. A sailor in an exposed position screamed as his eardrums burst. Then, with blood spurting from every orifice in his body, he was swept overboard by that tremendous blast. Watching the huge guns fire from the safety of that bridge, Hartmann told himself that surely nothing could survive that awesome salvo.

Huge columns of boiling, angry water went up to both port and startboard. A near miss threw one of the attackers high into the air. When the launch smacked down it broke in half immediately, then the chariot at her bow exploded. Seconds later there was nothing visible of her save the shattered debris bobbing up and down on the wild, rocking surface of the grey sea.

The *Tirpitz*'s guns boomed once more. The whole ship trembled. Another launch received a direct hit. It disintegrated immediately. One moment it was there; the next it was gone.

Howling Mad raged. Clenching his fists he jerked them at the sky, as if cursing God for having doomed his flotilla. But even in his rage he knew he would have to press home his attack. O'Rourke knew it, too. "All right, Chiefie!" he cried above that tremendous roar of the *Tirpitz*'s guns, "We're going in!"

"Ay, ay, sir," Harding replied loyally. He knew it was suicidal to attack now, but there was no alternative. He had spent a lifetime in the Royal Navy ever since he had joined up as a half-starved slum kid of 14. To die in the 'service of your country for the King-Emperor' had been drummed into him all that time. Now he must prepare to do just that.

"I'll take over, Chiefie," O'Rourke cried, "I'm a bit niftier than you."

"As you wish, sir." Looking at the young officer affectionately, Harding thought, why he's still wet behind the ears. Hasn't had any life to speak of. Now he's going for the chop. Aloud he said, "We might do it, sir, if we're a bit sharp on our toes."

"Of course we'll do it, Chiefie! Here we go." He felt the deck tremble violently beneath his feet as the motor-launch surged forward. Her bow tilted. Two great white combs of foam curved and fell to port and starboard. To their front, the *Tirpitz* was aflame with gun bursts from stem to stern. Great gouts of water hurtled to the grey sky. A solid white wall of flak and tracer fire awaited them. It seemed nothing could survive it.

Again the battleship's huge guns belched fire. Another launch was hit and yet another, disintegrating under those terrible hammer blows of the exploding shells, littering the sea with the pathetic debris of floats, pails, spars of wood and shattered bodies.

A burst of 20mm shells raked O'Rourke's craft. The bridge was struck. Next to O'Rourke, Harding screamed shrilly. He reeled back, holding a gnarled hand, covered with liver spots, to his eyes. "*Chiefie!*" O'Rourke cried, as Harding, gasping like a man who had just run a great race, sank to his knees. "What the devil—" He broke off and fought back the hot bile which threatened to choke him.

Slowly, very slowly, the old petty officer lowered his blood-soaked hands.

"Oh, my God!" O'Rourke gasped.

Where Harding's eyes had been there were now two empty pits, dripping blood-red gore.

"*Chiefie!*"

Harding groped a stanchion and righted himself with difficulty. "Don't worry . . . about me . . . sir," he panted, uttering each faint word with the greatest of efforts. "Just get the bastard . . . *Sink her!*"

"I will . . . I will, Chiefie!" O'Rourke shouted above the roar of the guns and the frantic chatter of the machine-guns. Suddenly he forgot all fear, all thoughts for his own safety. Now he was carried away by the old unreasoning lust to kill – for revenge. This time they'd get the *Tirpitz*! This time she wouldn't escape.

Another savage burst of fire raked the launch. Men fell everywhere. Poised in their chariot, the two Marines slumped dying. Other men lay crumpled on the deck like broken dolls cast aside by a careless child. Fire was beginning to lick up from the engine-room. A piece of shrapnel slammed into O'Rourke. He gasped with the sudden, sharp burning shock of it. Bone splintered, and his blood splattered the shattered deck in thick red gobs. His ears were filled with his own screams of pain. Urine and excreta streamed down his legs.

"Keep control!" he commanded himself. "Keep control, dammit!"

The *Tirpitz* loomed ever larger as the dying launch headed straight for it. Now, however, it seemed shrouded in a sudden wavering fog. Once it appeared to vanish altogether. Desperately O'Rourke blinded his eyes and it came back into focus. He knew he was dying, but it didn't matter now. All that mattered was to sink the monster in front of him. Behind O'Rourke, Chief Petty Officer Harding, who had once swaggered down the streets of Hull as a young buck after the Battle of Jutland, gave one last sad little sigh, closed his eyelids over those empty sockets and then sank gently to the deck, dead before he reached it.

Now the motor-launch with its crew of corpses and dying men was almost there in the dead ground under the lee of that massive hull. O'Rourke laughed crazily, though he knew this was the very end. In a moment it would be all over. But it didn't matter. Nothing mattered now except death to the *Tirpitz!*

For one last fleeting moment he smiled, as if at some secret joke. Then the motor-launch slammed into the hull of the *Tirpitz*. For a second or two the two ships, friend and foe, clung to each other like helpless lovers, the motor-launch's screws churning wildly, while the German sailors high above, their faces ashen and aghast, craned their necks and stared down at the dead and dying Englishmen. Then slowly, very slowly, the *Tirpitz* cast her adrift.

Too late! The tons of high explosive carried by the chariot and manned by its dead crew, suddenly exploded. On the *Tirpitz* there was a sudden, mind-rending shudder. It began amidships, worked its way aft, rattling through each compartment, flinging men to the deck, tossing them from bulkhead to bulkhead like snooker balls, showering them with masses of gear.

Dials splintered in the engine-room. Light bulbs popped. Steel stanchions bent, twisted and snapped as if they were made of plywood. Steam gushed upwards from the ruptured boilers. Half-naked stokers screamed shrilly as their flesh was seared by the boiling vapour. A petty officer blundered down between the boilers, the skin hanging from his burnt face like molten wax.

A series of massive shudders rocked the *Tirpitz*. The men who had rushed up in panic to the deck after the collision grabbed stanchions which vibrated crazily. The mighty battleship heaved from end to end. Aerials and davits came tumbling down. A life raft broke away and went over the side. A radio mast broke away from the superstructure, trailing angry blue sparks. Steel hawsers hissed through the air like silver whips and a sailor's scream was cut short as one of them sliced off his head, which rolled to the scuppers like an abandoned football.

On the bridge virtually all the warning lights were flashing. The glass of dials burst. The lights started to grow dim. Cursing and swearing, blood dripping from a jagged wound in his forehead, a chief petty officer armed with a wrench wrestled with the jammed telegraph.

"*Grosser Gott!*" Hartmann cursed, picking himself up from the littered deck to which he had been thrown by the impact of that great explosion. "What a mess!"

On the deck next to him was an officer who looked as if he had been split in two by a butcher's cleaver. Down by his navel the length of bright steel which had killed him protruded. Hartmann nearly started to heave. He caught himself in time. Like O'Rourke, he too had to keep control.

Men were running back and forth in panic down the already sloping deck. Obscene bubbles of trapped air were exploding on the surface to starboard. That meant the *Tirpitz* had been badly holed. The captain could hear the faint but frantic screams of those trapped below by the water. "Water-tight doors, close them!"

Dietz, bleeding from a shoulder wound and looking ashen, gasped, "Doing our best, sir. But we're having a hell—" He broke off abruptly. The great ship had begun to shudder violently once more. More of the superstructure started to snap off and crash to the packed deck below, crushing and killing those unfortunates who didn't get out of the way. A quick-firer tore away from the bolts fastening it to the upper deck and went tumbling downwards. The two senior officers knew what that meant. Water was flooding the hull at a tremendous rate. Soon the *Tirpitz*'s trim would go altogether and as the engines started to fail they would have no pumps to keep her on an even keel. The end was approaching.

"What are you going to do, sir?" Dietz asked in a hushed voice, holding his hand to his wounded shoulder, his fingers soaked in his own blood.

Before Hartmann could reply, the ship gave another great shudder and the engines stopped. Slowly but surely the *Tirpitz* started to list heavily to one side.

Hartmann knew the great adventure was over. Now all he could do was to save as many of his young men as he could before she went under. "I think," he said the words slowly and very reluctantly, as if he were finding it very difficult to utter them, "the time has come to abandon ship!"

Dietz looked at him aghast. "*Abandon ship!*" he echoed in an awed voice.

From below came a great groaning and creaking, eerie and frightening. It was the plates and bulk heads buckling one by one under the intense pressure of the seawater pouring into the ship. Abruptly what was left of the electric power vanished. The lights went out.

Hartmann knew the public address wouldn't work now. He turned and said to those officers and CPOs on the bridge who were still capable of moving, "Out on deck and tell the lads to abandon ship!"

They, too, were shocked but they hurried away to carry out his order.

Hartmann held his head, a tragic figure, Dietz thought. He knew the Hartmanns of this world. Like Langsdorff he would not live with his ship sunk. He wouldn't even attempt to find some reason for saving his own life.

Hartmann seemed to sense what his second-in-command was thinking, for he thrust out his hand and said in a quiet voice, "All right, Dietz, old friend, you may go—"

Again their conversation was interrupted by the sinking ship's dying shudders.

"I'll stay with you, sir," Dietz said stoutly.

"No, you must go . . . Help the men. They are all so young. They must survive. They are Germany's future."

But none of them were fated to survive.

Half a mile away in his battered, debris-littered launch, the dead sprawled all over the deck, the only craft of the attack flotilla afloat, Howling Mad Keith watched as the great ship's magazines started to explode. One muffled crump followed another. Smoke poured from the stricken ship in thick black mushrooms. Her bow started to slide under while her stern reared high into the dawn sky.

Suddenly her main magazine exploded. Five hundred yards away the awed survivors on the motor-launch felt the shock, as if someone had just punched them in the guts. The battleship's stern reared even higher into the sky, like the tower of some great steel cathedral. Slowly, inexorably, *Tirpitz* started to slide beneath the waves. The water leapt up greedily to receive her, only to recoil hastily, missing and spluttering as the waves came in contact with searing heat of red hot metal.

On the shattered bridge, Howling Mad felt no sense of triumph that they had dealt with the *Tirpitz* at last, only a sense of loss, of numbness.

With one last wild tumult of water the great battleship slid beneath the waves, leaving behind her an empty sea, save for a mass of floating debris – and the one survivor, crouching in a rubber float, sobbing, sobbing, sobbing as if his heart would break.

Slowly, very slowly, Howling Mad Keith raised his bloody hand to his barehead in salute.

ENVOI

They could now hear the first boom-boom of the band of the East Riding Yeomanry as it led the parade. The crowd's good-natured excitement mounted. Next to Fleming, the drunken soldier said, "It's 'Colonel Bogey' they're playing, 'Colonel Bogey'." Slurring the words, he began to sing, "*Where was the engine driver when the boiler bust? They found his bollocks – and the same to you*! . . . *Bollocks* . . ."

On the raised saluting dais next to the Lord Mayor of Hull, Churchill raised himself on his cane. Then he tugged at the tunic of his old regiment, the Fourth Hussars, which he had put on so that he could officially salute the Home Guard. The other senior officers did the same.

The band of the Yeomanry swung round the corner, their instruments gleaming in the weak winter sunshine. Now the street echoed and re-echoed to the blare of the brass and the thump of the big drum. The drum major thrust out his chest proudly and the crowd cheered.

Churchill grinned. Here and there civilians cried, "Good old Winnie!"

The Lord Mayor, with his chain of office dangling round his neck, frowned at such familiarity. Next to Fleming the soldier stopped singing and said out of the side of his mouth, "Here they come, all full of piss and vinegar! Look at them gongs and that webbing. I bet the poor old codgers have been bulling up for this parade for months."

Now, led by an old Brigadier on a white horse, the Home Guard, five abreast, swung round the corner, marching with fixed bayonet, their medals sparkling on their skinny chests. Filled with pride, faces set, they swung their arms like regulars. It was pretty obvious that they were enjoying the attention and the cheers of the crowd.

On the platform, Churchill looked happy as he ran his eyes along their ranks. Fleming guessed why. This standing-down parade was a tangible signal that the war was about won. All the same, might Churchill die at this moment of triumph? Nothing more had been heard of Commander Keith's flotilla ever since he had signalled that he was about to engage the *Tirpitz*. Despite the poor weather, Coastal Command had sent out two Sunderland flying boats to see if they could find out what had happened. So far they hadn't reported any sighting. As soon as the parade was over and Churchill was out of danger, Fleming would hurry back to the little naval HQ to find out if there was anything new.

There was the steady tread of hobnailed boots as rank after rank of the part-time soldiers marched past the saluting base. "Eyes left!" the company commanders barked, saluting and tucking their canes smartly under their left arms. Time and again Churchill raised his own hand to his cap in return. For such an old man he never seemed to weary of returning their salutes.

Then it happened.

Down the Humber the cry "*Hurrah!*" went up. At first it was faint and did not attract the attention of the crowd watching the great parade. Slowly, however, it started to rise in volume, as the dock workers in their oily dungarees and cloth caps took it up. Ships' sirens joined in, foghorns too. Outside the harbour-master's office a youngster in Trinity House uniform, complete with high stiff collar, jumped up and down excitedly, frantically turning a gas rattle.

On his white horse next to the saluting base the old Brigadier turned puce with anger. More and more of the crowd were turning their backs on the parade to stare at the stretch of dirty, oily water, wondering what was happening down there to cause such excitement.

Fleming followed their looks. It was then he saw it. A badly battered motor-launch, its superstructure riddled with bullet holes, and what could only be dead bodies lying stiffly under canvas on the debris-littered deck. It was Howling Mad Keith's boat, for there he stood on what remained of the bridge, a blood-stained towel wrapped around his wound, conning the craft to the anchorage.

But it wasn't the battered boat or the wounded Commander which caught Fleming's attention and made his heart beat faster. It was the flag attached to a make-shift mast, fluttering in the breeze that came across the water. It was black and bore a white skull-and-crossbones. It was the symbol of triumph, the customary sign that the boat had made a kill.

"Christ Almighty!" he blurted out, his old Etonian calm vanished. "They've done it. *They've sunk the Tirpitz*!"

The drunken soldier looked at him as if he had suddenly gone mad.

Up on the platform, Churchill let his right arm drop at last as the final company marched past. He smiled at Colville briefly and whispered out of the side of his mouth, "A brave lot, a brave lot!"

The Lord Mayor flushed with pride, as if the compliment was addressed to him personally.

Then, as the cheering died away and the battered craft started to tie up, with the overalled dockers rushing forward to help the wounded on to the quay, there were sudden tears in the old man's eyes. Somewhere the bells of an ambulance started to jingle urgently.

Churchill pulled himself together. There were other affairs of state to be taken care of. Hurriedly he shook the Lord Mayor's hand, leaned over the railing of the platform and called to the officer on the horse, "Splendid turnout, Brigadier! Absolutely!"

The old soldier puffed out his bemedalled chest and swung the Prime Minister such a tremendous salute that he nearly fell off his white horse. "Thank you sir," he cried as the horse bucked with surprise.

The PM turned to Colville and whispered, "Well, you know what they say, Colville? From Hell, Hull and Halifax, let the Good Lord preserve us. Let us hie back to London!"

Colville smiled and then they were gone.

Operation Sink the *Tirpitz* was over.